P9-CDZ-507

THE LONG TRAINS ROLL

THE LONG TRAINS ROLL

by S_{TEPHEN} $W.$ M_{EADER}

ILLUSTRATED BY
EDWARD SHENTON

HARCOURT, BRACE & WORLD, INC.
NEW YORK

J.4.64

THE LONG TRAINS ROLL

Sometimes you wake up in bed and hear the mournful hoot of a freight locomotive, miles away across the sleeping country. Or you feel the throb of earth-shaking wheels, beating out their rhythm on the rails. All night long they roll—the red-ball freights and the rocketing passenger limiteds—going about their vast and lonely business, moving a billion ton-miles between dark and dawn. They are the lifeblood of a mighty nation. Whether America is asleep or awake, food and fuel, merchandise and people never cease traveling to every corner of the land along the steel arteries of the rails.

I

Carrying his brimming milk pail, Randy MacDougal stopped halfway between the barn and the kitchen door. The sky to the east, above the wooded ridges, was pink and gold. The sun was not quite high enough to be seen from the slope where the farmhouse stood, but it already shed a glittering halo on the summit of Big Calico, lifting like a great, shaggy beast above the clearing. The chill of dawn was still in the air and long rivers of mist drifted up the valley. It was a fine mountain morning.

Randy was whistling "Casey Jones" as he kicked open the screen door and set his milk to cool on the bench in the entry. He washed his hands at the sink, dried them on a roller towel and gave his mother's plump waist an exuberant squeeze. "Hiya, Mom," he grinned, ducking the swing of her arm. "How's about some breakfast?"

"It's on the table, yon, if ye but had eyes to see it," she answered. "Your father's done eating, an' Jeannie'll be down in a wee bit. Be at your porridge now, while it's hot."

Randy was pouring milk on his oatmeal when his father's burly body filled the doorway. "Come, lad," Big Ross

MacDougal rumbled. He fished his thick railroad watch from his pocket. "Ye've got five minutes—no more. The six-ten's on her way up the grade right now."

Jean whisked down the stairs and pulled up a chair opposite her brother. She was nineteen—two years older than Randy—and considered herself a grown-up. She had a steady job as a secretary in the Gaptown car shops, while Randy was still in high school and could work only in the three summer months.

The boy finished his oatmeal, bacon and eggs, and gulped down a second glass of milk. Jean's breakfast was more dainty—fruit juice, toast and a cup of coffee. They got up from the table together, within their father's time limit.

"Don't forget your lunch-box, lad," Mrs. MacDougal warned. "An' be sure ye're off the track when the trains go by."

Randy laughed. "Fine advice for a born railroader!" he teased her. "Might as well tell Pop to be sure he's in the cab when he opens up the throttle on old 722!"

The starter of the car ground away outside and then the motor caught with a stuttering roar. Randy ran out and swung into the back seat as Jean guided the battered 1938 model out of the dooryard and down the stony hill road.

4

"You going all the way in with us?" the girl asked over her shoulder.

"Reckon not," Randy replied. "Stop at the head o' the path an' I'll hop a down freight to the yard."

Jean put on the brakes as she neared the next curve and the car pulled over to the side of the road. The boy jumped out and waved good-by to his father and sister. A moment later he was plunging down a steep trail through a jungle of rhododendron and mountain laurel. He kept one hand ahead of him to hold the smooth green leaves out of his eyes, and sniffed the fragrance of the dewy woods. The path wound down the rough hillside for two hundred yards and suddenly emerged at the edge of the railroad cut.

Randy paused a moment as he always did when he reached this spot. Spread before him was the four-track main line of the railroad, climbing in a long loop to the crest of the divide, where Calico Gap cut its black notch against the sky. From where he stood there were four trains in sight. Right below him a string of eighty empty gondolas and oil tankers was sweating up the grade behind a pair of grunting freight hogs. Across the valley, on the next higher curve, a heavy mixed freight was drifting down the mountain. Over on the third track a solid block of seventy black tank

5

cars clanked eastward with the helper engine loafing behind the caboose. And far down toward the smoke of Gaptown a big westbound passenger train was doubleheading up the rise.

He could feel the throb of powerful drivers shaking the hillside like the beat of a giant's pulse. A big share of all the continent's east-west traffic rolled past this spot—the only rail crossing in a hundred miles of mountain wall.

Just above him, to the west, the right-of-way climbed in a vast arc, hugging the side of a natural bowl, then swinging back to the right around the shoulder of Big Calico and vanishing from sight in the direction of the Gap. He could see the smoke of puffing engines up there, a cloud of white against the grim outline of Blacksnake Mountain, on the opposite side of the gorge.

Randy drew a deep, exultant breath. Just looking at that mighty enterprise and knowing he had a part in it—even the modest part of a section hand—made him feel ten feet tall!

But this wasn't getting him to work. The mixed freight he had seen coming down around the loop was drawing nearer now. He scrambled down the rocky side of the cut, crossed over the two westbound tracks, and waited. The block signal on the down line showed clear, for the hotshot string of oil tankers had already passed the Gaptown yards. The approaching freight was slowing down now, bucking the air on the one per cent grade. No exhaust came from the stacks of the two big mountain-type locomotives. The fireman on the helper engine had crawled back over the coal to cut her loose, and as they passed Randy they were moving at an easy fifteen miles an hour.

The first quarter of the train clanked by and the boy saw a familiar figure swaying along the footboard on top of a tall boxcar. It was Joe Roan, an old friend of his, working as head-end brakeman. Randy sprinted along the track, grabbed a hand-bar and swung himself in against the car, with his feet reaching for the stirrup iron. A moment later he was up beside Roan, sitting on the car roof with an arm hooked around the handbrake shaft.

"Hiya, kid." The brakeman grinned. "How goes it? Ain't seen you in a couple o' weeks. Still think it's fun bein' a gandy dancer?"

"Sure," said Randy. "Why not? Don't you know it's the section hands that keep the railroad running?"

Joe Roan laughed heartily at that. "I always figgered it was us freight shacks," he said. "Maybe countin' in the hoggers an' tallowpots that shove steam, up there ahead—an'

7

the towermen an' dispatchers—an' a division super or two. But I'll admit we wouldn't do much highballin' without that ol' roadbed under us."

Randy watched the helper engine let go and pull out ahead. "What's your haul this morning?" he asked idly.

"Mixed, out o' Detroit an' Toledo. Mostly war stuff, I reckon, 'cause we got a red-ball through from Pittsburgh. There's a road dick back there in the crummy, too. Better not let him catch you deadheadin'."

Randy glanced back, but the caboose was half a mile behind and there was nobody on top of the cars. He had been raised on rail slang and had no difficulty understanding Roan's lingo. The news that a railroad detective was aboard the caboose, or "crummy," did not disturb him. They often rode the preference freights that carried war supplies these days, keeping an eye out for possible sabotage. It wasn't likely that they would make trouble for a legitimate railroad worker getting a free ride to his job.

"You think he saw me climb on?" Randy asked.

"Oh, sure. Ben Small may be slow on his feet but he don't miss much," said Joe. "He's sittin' up there in the cupola an' he'll ask a few questions about you when I go back."

"Who's Ben Small?" Randy inquired. "I thought I knew

8

most o' the dicks on the mountain division."

"He's a queer dope. Big as a house. Must weigh three hundred pounds. He always looks half asleep an' he's got a little, high, squeaky voice that don't seem to go with his size. They say he's a whiz at catchin' criminals, though. Come up here from Jersey a couple o' months ago."

"I guess the management thinks this is a pretty important stretch o' track, up here in the Gap," Randy mused. "It would do some real damage if the Germans could block the high iron, wouldn't it?"

"Gosh! I'll say it would! An' it's not only the management thinks so. The Army an' the F.B.I. are mighty anxious about what goes on 'round here. Remember a couple o' years back, when a bunch o' spies landed on the coast in a rubber boat?"

"Yeah, I read about it," Randy answered.

"Well," the young brakeman went on, "when they caught 'em, those guys had maps that showed three or four places where they could do the best job o' slowin' up the war effort. New York harbor was one—an' some o' these airplane plants—an' ol' Calico Gap, where the big freights haul through! Even over in Berlin they know about this neck o' the woods."

Randy nodded. He had it on the tip of his tougue to repeat a rumor he had heard the day before—that a platoon
of soldiers was secretly camped in the woods, up on the
crest of Blacksnake, guarding the railroad's main line. But he
remembered the poster on the wall of the section house—
the big-eared caricature of Hitler and the warning, "Loose
Talk Costs Lives." He thought of his two brothers in Army
khaki, doing their railroad work in Africa and India now.
And he closed his mouth tight. There was no reason to tell
all he had heard, even to an old acquaintance like Joe Roan.

The freight was rumbling over switch-points, moving
more and more slowly as it rolled into the upper end of
the yard. Randy could see the low, gray-painted shanty that
housed the tools and equipment of the section gang. Two or
three figures were already gathered by the door, and even
from a quarter of a mile away the boy recognized the broad
shoulders and gorilla arms of old Dan Leary, the section
foreman.

"Well, Joe," he told the brakeman, "I'll be seeing you
around. Don't miss any switches."

He swung down the ladder, looked forward and back
to make sure there was nothing coming, and dropped lightly
off on the rock ballast between the ties. The right-of-way

was wider here, where the rails branched off in an intricate pattern of tracks. The boy picked his way across, waiting now and then for a clanging switch-engine and its string of boxcars to go bustling past. Over on the westbound side, a black brute of a 4-8-4 locomotive rolled through a switch onto the main iron and backed up to the pilot of the road engine on a long freight. It was a helper, getting ready to doublehead the "Buckeye" hotshot over the grade.

Randy stopped for a better look, but the number on the engine wasn't "722." His father would still be busy with the oil can, down in the roundhouse, while his ashcat got steam up.

The deep bellow of the car-shop whistle, a mile down the valley, shattered the morning air as the boy skipped across the last track. It was seven o'clock—time for all good section hands to be at work. He joined the little group in front of the shanty and answered their "good-mornings." Dan Leary was unlocking the door while the last stragglers hurried up.

"All right, b'ys," the gray-haired Irishman roared cheerily. "Lend a hand wid the stuff, an' be lively. Load up the rail-car an' the trailer. We got a big day's wurrk ahead av us."

It was always the same with old Dan—a big day's work

ahead was something he relished. Now he looked about him at his crew with a good-natured grimace. It was a different kind of section gang from the ones he had started with, forty years ago. Here were none of the strong-backed immigrants, hard drinkers and rough fighters, that he had bossed in those earlier days. Randy followed the man's glance around the group and knew what he was thinking. There were three youngsters in the gang—boys like himself, of seventeen or under. Willing enough, and quick to learn, but still short of muscle. Three others were women of assorted ages. And the five remaining members of the crew were quiet-mannered men, some elderly, some with physical handicaps that kept them out of military service.

Under the foreman's orders they began passing out picks and shovels, claw-bars and tamping bars, spike mauls and spanners. The tools were loaded on the gasoline-driven railcar and its trailer and the gang climbed aboard, sitting on a pair of narrow, outward-facing benches. The engine began to sputter and chug.

"Howld fast, all av yez!" Dan Leary bellowed. "We're off!"

Northeast and southwest run the long, parallel ridges of the Appalachian chain. The White Mountains and the Adirondacks, the Alleghenies and the Cumberlands, the Blue Ridge and the Great Smokies—1300 miles of rock and coal and iron, furred with pine and hemlock, oak and ash and hickory. For 150 years the mountain barrier walled in the colonies along the seacoast. Until the bold men who crossed—the men in fur caps and deerskin hunting-shirts, with long rifles in their hands—brought back news of a vast continent beyond. Then the settlers began to move, pouring through the notches and the gaps. They went over on horseback and with wagons, and they voyaged down westward-flowing rivers in flatboats, and they built America. But the mountains are still there. The gaps and notches are still the only land gateways through the Appalachian wall.

II

There was a clear block and no upgrade trains in sight as the section car cut over to the westbound Number Two track. Even with its heavy load and the trailer behind it, the rail-car's sturdy little power plant trundled them along at ten miles an hour. Randy and young Mike Hubka, one of the other boys in the crew, were back on the trailer, squatting on a pile of tools.

"Where are we s'posed to be workin' today?" Mike asked. "It's goin' to be hot, an' I hope we find some shade."

"Not much chance o' that," grinned Randy. "You'll probably get an all-day sun-bath. I heard the old man say we're going to pack ballast up in the cut."

"Oh—oh!" the other boy groaned. He was heavily built and summer weather made him perspire.

The grade stiffened after a mile or two. As the rail-car's speed dropped, a twelve-car passenger train thundered by them on the outside track. Randy looked up at the clean lines of the big Pacific-type engine and her towering 80-inch drivers. That was his ambition—to handle the throttle of a crack flier on one of the road's famous western runs. The fireman sat disdainfully on his lofty perch and did not glance at the boys. Then the long, sleek cars rolled by, and finally came the chugging mountain freight-hog that pushed them from behind. It was his father's engine.

"Yippee!" yelled Randy. "Hiya, Buck!"

At the window appeared the grinning, coal-smeared face of Buck Weeks, regular tallowpot in the cab of 722.

"Hi, kid!" he called jovially. "Two bits says we'll beat yuh to the Gap!"

Then he was gone in a cloud of dust and cinders. Mike looked back down the track and nudged Randy with his elbow. "We better get to the next switch quick," he said. "There's a freight catchin' up on us."

Randy nodded. "They're still a long way back," he answered. "But it's half a mile to the cutover. We'd better pile off an' lighten the load."

The two boys jumped from the trailer and trotted along the ballast beside it. Dan Leary had seen the freight too. He shouted an order and more of the crew left the rail-car. With its burden reduced, the little gas engine picked up speed. Soon it had left the panting section hands behind.

"No use killin' ourselves," an old-timer growled. "We can take our time walkin' up there now."

He crossed over to the embankment beyond the Number One track and led the way along a footpath. "That's what ye git for havin' new-fangled gadgets on the right-o'-way," he told the boys. "Back in the old days we could snake a hand-car off one track onto another in two shakes of a lamb's tail. We could make 'em hum, too, when we wanted. 'Long about 1910 there was four of us goin' to a dance down the valley. All broadbacks, an' all used to pumpin' the handles. We swiped a hand-car an' started at eight o'clock with a down freight highballin' right on our heels. Well, sir, we got that durn little track-flea goin' so fast the rails was smokin'. Seven miles it was to the Bellowsburg sidin' an' we sailed in there at eight-ten, right on the advertised. Couldn't stop, neither. Went clean through the end o' the freight shed an' tore our pants so bad none of us got to the dance. But I reckon we set a record that night."

Another of the gray-haired veterans in the crew snickered to himself. "You must ha' been a durn sight spryer'n you be now," he told the hand-car expert. "An' I bet nobody was any gladder'n you when the road give us power-cars."

"Mebbe so," the other rejoined testily. "All I say is, we was he-men in the ol' days. An' there ain't many such left."

Mike winked at Randy as the boys left the arguing an-

17

cients behind. "They don't even know we're in a war," he chuckled. "Wonder where they think all the he-men have gone to."

The siding where Leary and the rest of the gang had stopped was well up the grade at the beginning of the big curve. Under the foreman's orders they were already walking up the track with their tools when the boys arrived. They picked up a ballast fork apiece and followed.

Packing ballast was a simple enough job, and Randy had got the knack of it in his few weeks on the gang. It was a matter of pulling the loose stone out from around the tie-ends, making sure there had been no settling of ballast underneath, raising the tie a little if necessary and adding fresh rock, then replacing the ballast and tamping it firm. Occasionally they would come to a spike that needed driving down or a flange-bolt that had to be tightened.

There was enough variety to the job to keep it from being monotonous, and most of it was good, hard exercise for back and arm muscles. The women worked right along with the men on all but the heaviest tasks.

Big Dan Leary's eagle eye took in every tie and spike, every rail and rail joint. He kept the crew alert and on their toes without driving them. Randy had been a little awed by his bull voice and fiercely jutting eyebrows at first. But he knew Leary had the reputation of being the best "king snipe" on the division and it was something of an honor to be in his gang.

There was nothing lazy about the section boss. He could move like a cat, for all his years, and if there was a heavy job like lifting a tie to be done he was the first to put his weight on the bar.

He never swore at the gang or bullied them. But his Irish blarney got more work out of them than harsher methods. "Ah, now, Molly," he would tell one of his feminine charges, "ye'll do it prettier an' save yer back from achin' if ye swing the shovel this way." And he would take the scoop out of her hands and demonstrate the easy, graceful motion.

Every minute of the day he kept a watchful eye on traffic up and down the rails. It was a point of pride with him that he had never lost a man in forty years on the road, and he saw to it that his track-watchers were always on the alert. The gang was warned in plenty of time to lay down their tools and get clear of the tracks when a train was coming.

Those passing trains gave the section hands plenty of rest periods. Randy, who had lived close to the right-of-way all his life, never ceased to marvel at the volume of traffic moving in these war days. A dozen times, that morning, he saw the white-flagged engines of special trains roar past. Some of them were long strings of heavy flatcars, loaded with anti-aircraft guns, tanks and Army tractors—grotesque-shaped monsters under their tarpaulin covers. Some were fifteen-car trains of passenger coaches, with disheveled boys in khaki crowded at every window.

Once a special freight came rumbling down the mountain, its grimy boxcars guarded by a double crew of brakemen, and soldiers in uniform riding the caboose. There were no warning signs with the word "Explosives!" on those cars, but Randy knew they were loaded with shells and heavy bombs for the armies overseas.

Then there was all the regular scheduled traffic of the road, running in long trains and double sections—the smooth-gliding Pullmans and the endlessly rolling freights.

Mike and Randy played a sort of game, seeing who could count up the biggest number of railroad names on the passing boxcars, tankers and gondolas. Any single train of mixed freight might have cars in it from twenty or thirty different lines.

"How many you got now?" Mike would ask jealously.

"Me—I make it sixty-eight."

"Sixty-nine." Randy grinned. "I bet you missed that T.P.&W. and thought it was another Texas & Pacific."

"T.P.&W.—what the heck road is that?"

"It's a freight line in Illinois—Toledo, Peoria & Western. See? You learn something every day!"

"Hm!" Mike snorted. "I saw the T.P. okay, but there must ha' been a dirt spot over the W."

"Seventy, now," said Randy with a chuckle. "While you were talking there was an old Cumberland Valley car went by."

"Shucks, you know durn well that's a Pennsy line!" Mike replied with heat. "No fair countin' a car they just forgot to paint!"

These arguments were never settled, but Randy enjoyed the game. It gave him a sense of the bigness of his country —the enormous movement of goods over far-flung ribbons of steel—all converging here in the busy rush of freight through the Gap.

Late in the forenoon, when the sun was blazing nearly overhead and fulfilling Randy's promise, the boys heard a motor droning in the sky. The plane that came slowly over was painted Army olive drab and bore the Air Force insignia. It was a high-wing, single-engine monoplane, with fixed landing gear. And it was flying so low that they could see the pilot looking down at them from the cockpit.

"That's an old O-46—Army observation job," Mike Hubka announced. He wanted to be a flier and had made a study of planes. Randy was impressed.

"How could you tell?" he asked enviously.

"That's an easy one," Mike answered. "She's about the only ship that has that curve in the trailin' edge o' the wing. Makes her look like a dragon-fly. She's been flyin' up an' down the line here quite a few times lately."

Randy watched the plane swing south, climbing along the curve, then buzz away out of sight around the shoulder of Big Calico. Was the pilot merely out on a practice flight, or was this another evidence of the Army's interest in this particular stretch of railroad? Without putting his thoughts into words he filed the idea away with other bits of information he had picked up.

When the distant blast of the noon whistle came up to them from Gaptown, Leary peered at his old-fashioned watch and gave the order to knock off for lunch. Randy and Mike took their boxes across the tracks and found a shady spot under the trees. As they ate they could look off down the twisting valley of the Blacksnake River. The woods were the deep, rich green of early summer, and the long ranges slanted away to the southwest, fading to misty blue in the distance.

"Sort o' pretty, ain't it?" said Mike with his mouth full of pie.

"Sure is," Randy answered. "It looks peaceful but mighty wild, too. No farms—not even a house in sight from here. If it wasn't for the noise the trains make you might think you were back in the old days—when the hunters went over the mountain after buffalo, an' the Indians came over after scalps."

"Gee!" Mike eyed him with respect. "You know a lot about hist'ry an' stuff, don't you? How'd you get all that dope?"

"From my dad, mostly. He's read a lot o' books, an' when he first came over from Scotland—he was only a kid then, younger'n I am—he liked this country and learned a heap about it. We took hikes around on the mountain when I was little. He showed me places where the Indian trails used to run, an' where settlers' cabins had been burned down in the raids."

"Gee!" said Mike again. "Air raids? When was all that?"

23

"No, no—Indian raids. They happened 'most two hundred years ago. Come on, old Dan'll be wanting us back on the track."

They climbed the embankment, waited for a down-bound string of tank-cars to clank past, and joined the rest of the gang. The morning breeze had died and the air hung heavy and sultry over the mountain. Shimmery heat waves danced above the polished surfaces of the rails. The sweat rolled down their faces and stained their work-shirts as they swung their picks and shovels.

About 3:30 in the afternoon a huge white thunderhead appeared over the summit of Big Calico. Watching beside the track as a freight-train passed, Randy saw the cloud lift and blacken. It covered the sun and threw a dark shadow over the grade.

"The day's near done," Leary observed. "An' there's no use gettin' ourselves soaked to the skin. Pick up the tools an' we'll be movin'."

There was only one way to get the rail-car and trailer over to the eastbound tracks, and that was to carry them. With the whole gang lifting on the hand-holds the two vehicles were moved in a few minutes. Then the equipment was piled aboard and they took their places on the cars. It was none too soon. As big Dan started the engine a terrific clap of thunder shook the mountain.

It took only a moment to pick up speed on the down-grade. They could hear a sudden wind screaming through the Gap and see the tree-tops bend as they flew by. Then the first big drops lashed down and the rain came in gray sheets on the heels of the wind.

They had to stop to open a switch at the head of the yard, and Randy dashed ahead to do it. After the car chugged through he closed it again and jumped on the trailer with water streaming from his arms and clothes.

Drenched and shivering, they all crowded into the section house as soon as Leary got the door open. It was dry inside and the air had been heated all day by sun on the iron roof. The shivering stopped and after a moment they could laugh at the wetting they had received. To the boys it made small difference, but the women looked so woebegone and bedraggled that Dan Leary did his best to cheer them up. "Too bad, Mrs. Clancy," he clucked sympathetically. "I'm afeared ye can't wear that handsome gown to church this Sunday. A shame, too—it's so becomin' to ye, wid the pink in yer cheeks from the rain an' all!"

The roar of the deluge on the roof dropped to a faint

patter and suddenly ceased. When Randy stuck his head out
the door the sun was glistening on the drip from the eaves.
He looked down the yard toward town and saw a man approaching, picking his way along the ties and holding an
umbrella that hid his face. From the careful way he stepped,
the boy knew he wasn't used to walking track.

Most of the section gang had taken their lunch-pails and
started for home when the stranger reached the shed. Randy
and Dan Leary were still standing in the doorway watching
the streams of water run off along the ditches. The man
stopped in front of them, folded his umbrella and smiled.
He was above middle height and his body looked bulky
under the old raincoat he wore. He was about forty-five,
Randy thought.

" 'Afternoon." He nodded to Leary. "Are you the section
foreman?"

"That's right," said old Dan.

"I've been hired and assigned to your gang. Got my papers
here from the Maintenance-of-Way office."

While Leary glanced over the rumpled sheets, Randy
took further stock of the newcomer. He had a pale face and
pale, watery eyes, behind thick glasses, but his smile was
pleasant enough. The boy thought his hands looked white

26

and soft for a manual laborer.

"Ever done any track work before?" the boss asked.

"No, I'm afraid not. Most of my jobs have been inside."
The man smiled vaguely. "But you'll find me strong enough
and willing to learn."

"Okay, we take what we can get, these days," Leary
grunted. "Be here at seven o'clock tomorrer mornin'."

The stranger nodded, shot a glance at Randy, and walked
off down the yard.

"Queer birds they send us." The old man grinned. "Well,
I'll be seein' ye, boy."

Randy picked his way across the network of tracks and
waited for an up-bound freight to give him a lift as far as the
home path. The afternoon sun felt good on his shoulders,
and he found his shirt and overalls were nearly dry again.
He looked back to where the departing stranger was now
no more than a brown dot against a line of boxcars. Funny,
what would bring a man of that type to get a section job
when the defense plants were paying twice as much. Oh,
well, the boy shrugged, it was no worry of his. A string of
empty refrigerator cars slowed down for the kicker engine
to couple on behind, and Randy climbed aboard. He'd be
home in time to get the chores done early tonight.

The trains stop at little stations and sweating, grinning boys in GI khaki crowd the open windows. They are bleary-eyed and tousled from sleeping in cinder-filled coaches, but they sing and shout and whistle at the girls. They try to buy sandwiches and cokes and candy-bars, or mail a post-card home. Then the engine snorts, and the wheels begin to roll, and they're on their way again. All over America the troops are moving—from induction centers to training camps and on to the embarkation points. Carrying a million soldiers a month, hard-worked railroad crews do their best for those boys. They know there are some of them who won't come back.

III

When Randy reached the section house next morning, the new man was already on hand. Dan Leary introduced him to his fellow workers as they arrived. "This here's Lew Burns, from over Pittsburgh way. Goin' to see how he likes gandy dancin'."

The gang moved up into the cut and went to work. Old Dan watched the baffled expression on the stranger's face as he fumbled for a shovel and followed the others uncertainly.

"Take yer time, mister," he advised. "Ye'll learn quick enough. Just keep an eye on young Randy, here. He ain't a bad section hand, an' he'll show ye the trick av it."

Burns gave him that watery-eyed smile and tried dutifully to imitate all that Randy did. The boy didn't mind his new role of instructor. In fact he was inwardly proud that old Dan had picked him out. Soon he had the beginner doing the simpler jobs without too much clumsiness.

It was another warm day and, as the sun climbed higher, Burns began to feel the heat. He laid his coat on the rail-car, took off his felt hat and mopped his forehead. "I expect this will be good for me, but I'm really not used to it," he puffed in apology.

"You ought to dress different for a job like this," Randy told him. He eyed the man's wool trousers and wilting stiff collar with disapproval. "Didn't you know it was going to be hot out here on the line?"

"I suppose I should have." Burns nodded. "But I've been a bookkeeper so long I'd really forgotten."

He looked at the puffy palms of his hands, where blisters were beginning to form, and smiled so ruefully that Randy was sorry for him. When noontime came he pointed out a shady spot and invited the older man to eat lunch with him.

Burns sighed as he eased his bulky body down on a bed of ferns. "Perhaps you can tell me something about this job," he said. "You see I don't know much about railroads. Do the section gangs keep at it all the time, or only when there's something that needs fixing?"

Randy stared at him. Such ignorance was to be pitied.

"They work on every section of every railroad, every day," the boy explained. "You take a stretch o' track like this, with a train going by every five minutes, an' there's always some wear an' tear to be fixed. Spikes get loose, or the roadbed washes a little, or a side-plate lets go where the rails come together. There are track walkers out, night an' day, looking for anything that might go wrong. An' they report to the section boss. My dad's an engineer, an' he often says the railroads couldn't run a week if it wasn't for the section gangs."

Burns seemed impressed. "The rails look so heavy and strong," he said, "I guess I thought they could stand anything."

"Look," Randy told him. "Here comes a coal train down the grade. Watch the rails while she goes over. There—see the track settle an' rise? That's heavy rail—131 pounds o' steel to the yard—an' solid rock ballast. But when a big freight hog an' a string o' loaded cars come along, something has to give. The rails spring an inch or two every time a truck goes over 'em."

They finished eating and Burns filled a pipe and lighted it. "I expect you're wondering," he said, between puffs, "how a man like me happened to get into a job like this. As I said before, I've worked in offices most of my life. I was a bookkeeper at a warehouse in Pittsburgh until last week. Then I figured I ought to be doing something more useful—helping win the war, and all that. I tried to get employment in a couple of munitions plants, but my eyes aren't very good and they told me I couldn't do close work. So then I thought of the railroads and came up here. Do you think I'll be any good at it—after I get hardened up, I mean?"

He sounded so wistfully eager that Randy wanted to cheer him up. "Sure!" he replied. "You can't expect to learn everything the first day, but you ought to make a first-class hand in another month."

They were working on the eastbound tracks that afternoon, moving steadily up the grade at two or three hundred feet an hour. A white-flag engine came down around the curve pulling a long train of old coaches—fifteen of them Randy counted as he waited beside the track. They were loaded with troops. Most of the windows were open and the soldiers who waved and shouted as they rolled past were a fair cross-section of Young America. There were rangy Texans and wiry boys from the South, big, towheaded Scandinavians from the Northwest and city youngsters, bronzed and toughened by months of training.

Their ties were off and their collars open in the heat, and their faces were dirty from long travel. Some napped with their heads back and mouths wide. Some moved restlessly up and down the crowded aisles. Jamming every available inch of space were packs and rifles and steel helmets—the full equipment of an infantry outfit on the move.

"Quite a sight, isn't it?" said Burns, as the tail end of the train went by. "How many men do you think they carry in each car?"

"I don't know—somewhere between sixty and eighty, I reckon," Randy replied. "Those old coaches haven't got as many seats as the new ones, but there must be close to a thousand men on that one train."

Half an hour later another troop train came through, and right behind it was a third—twelve cars in one and fourteen in the other. Randy started up the embankment after the last car passed, and glanced back at Burns to see why he was not following. The new man had pulled a little red-covered notebook out of his pocket and was writing something in it with a stub of pencil. He looked up at the boy and smiled apologetically.

"I'm so absent-minded," he said, "I have to write reminders to myself. I wanted to be sure to buy a work-shirt like yours, so I made a note of it."

"What a man!" thought Randy to himself. "Just about as helpless as a baby."

The monotony of the job was broken suddenly, a little after three o'clock. Dan Leary had gone a couple of rail-lengths up the track and now his deep voice called all hands to action.

"Come a-runnin'!" he roared. "Got a sprung iron here. You, Mike an' Bill—bring up the rail-tongs. Randy, get ready to flag anythin' comin' down. Ye'll find a couple o' torpedoes in the signal box, an' get up the line as far as ye can. The rest of ye bring yer claw-bars an' start pullin' spikes."

Randy threw a hasty glance up the mountain, made sure there was no eastbound train in sight, and raced for the rail-car. He opened the lid of the box and grabbed up a red flag and two signal torpedoes. Then he started sprinting up the track. As he passed the little knot of workers he caught sight of a heavy freight coming out of the Gap and starting down the long curve.

He had done some running on the high-school track team but this was different. Here he was climbing a two per cent grade, his heavy work shoes slipping clumsily on the rock ballast. If possible he knew he ought to give the freight engineer a half mile to stop in.

He lengthened his stride and ran steadily, his breath coming in painful gasps until he got his second wind. The telegraph poles dropped behind, one after another, and he counted them off—twenty . . . twenty-one . . . twenty-two . . . only three more to go. The freight was less than a mile away now. He put all the speed he could muster into that last hundred yards. As he passed the twenty-fifth pole he paused to clamp one torpedo to the rail, then stumbled on a short distance and placed the other.

He was dizzy and his chest was heaving as he stepped back off the track and started waving the red flag. The big locomotive roared nearer—almost on top of him—and there was no sign from the cab that his warning had been heeded. Desperately he wiped the sweat out of his eyes and peered upward. Where was that fool of a hogger?

Then—*bang!* The first torpedo went off, followed quickly by the second. The engineer's head popped suddenly from the window and air brakes hissed and squealed as the long freight began to slow down. When the train finally groaned to a stop, the pilot of the head engine was a scant hundred yards above the break in the track.

Randy felt limp all over. He heaved a shaky sigh of relief and started back down the grade. Just above him, on top of the train, the head-end brakeman was waving his arms, signaling the men at the rear. Looking back, the boy saw a tiny speck drop off the caboose and run up the track.

"Gotta get a flagman out," the brakeman said. "Number

60's only five minutes back of us. There's a T.B. back there by the crummy. I reckon the Big Ox'll put the word through to the Gap. Yeah—there he goes now."

Randy knew the "Big Ox" meant the freight conductor, otherwise known as the "Brains." The "T.B." was one of the telephone boxes, placed at intervals of a mile along the main iron.

"What's wrong down there?" the brakeman inquired, and when Randy told him he shook his head. "Too much rail trouble lately," he said. "One let go over the other side o' the hump this afternoon. Spread a dozen empties over the ground but there was nobody hurt. They sent the big hook up from Ramsville. Prob'ly got it about clear by now."

He settled himself on the top of the car with his long legs dangling over and helped himself to a chew of tobacco. He was a grizzled, leathery-faced man of fifty or more, and the brim of his battered hat was turned up fore and aft at a rakish angle.

"Me, I'm a boomer," he announced with a certain amount of pride. "I've worked on thirty roads an' done everything from poundin' brass to liftin' transportation on a varnish run. I've been ashcat, shack an' runner on lines from here to Mexico. But I was brakin' over the Gap in the last war an'

36

when this one come along I figgered this was where I was needed."

He paused to shoot an amber stream from the corner of his mouth. "Movin' freight like we do through here, it's no wonder the iron takes a beatin'," he continued. "Some talk about sabotage every time there's a sprung rail, but not me. If you double the traffic over the track you gotta expect some wear an' tear. Ain't that right, sonny?"

Randy replied that he thought it probably was. "Sorry, but I've got to be getting back," he told the boomer. "We'll be giving you a go-ahead pretty quick. So long, now."

He jogged down the track till he reached the tender of the big road engine. The engineer was leaning out, looking ahead.

"Hey, punk!" he yelled as the boy went by below. "Next time you flag a train, give us room to stop!"

Randy's gorge rose. "All right, hogger," he called back wrathfully. "Next time they let you run something bigger'n a yard goat, keep your eye on the track—or maybe you wouldn't know what a red flag meant if you saw it!"

He went on, unmindful of the loud abuse that poured from the cab. The section gang had the new rail in place and most of the spikes driven. Dan Leary was tightening plate-bolts with the spanner as Randy came up.

"All right, b'y," he panted. "Wan jiffy now an' ye can give that hoghead the high-sign."

Randy grinned and went a few yards up the line, waiting for the section foreman's word. When it came he lifted his arms in the highball signal. There was a belch of smoke from the locomotive's stack, the deep cough of the exhaust, and the freight began to move.

As the boy expected, the engineer was hanging out of his cab, still red-faced with rage. Randy walked back unconcernedly to Leary's side.

"Friend o' yours?" he asked, jerking a thumb toward the approaching engine.

". . . blankety-blank dumb track-louse!" the hogger was shouting, when Leary's mighty bellow drowned him out.

"Quiet, ye blitherin' ape!" the old section boss roared. He had a spike-maul in his fist and he brandished it so menacingly that the engineer ducked back inside his cab. The whole gang joined in the hoot of laughter that followed the engine down the line.

"Now phwat d'ye suppose started that?" big Dan asked mildly. There was a twinkle in his eyes as he watched Randy pick up a shovel and start industriously to work.

When four o'clock came, the crew carried their tools back to the rail-car and loaded up for the return trip. Burns was obviously tired. His feet were dragging and his neck and forearms were burned a bright lobster red. The stiff collar had long since wilted to a rag and been discarded.

He looked at his blistered hands ruefully. "I'm afraid I won't earn my wages until I get some calluses," he said.

"You did okay today," the boy assured him. "An' the quickest way to toughen up is to stick to it, even if your hands hurt. I'll see you Monday—an' say—don't forget that work-shirt you're going to buy!"

Dan Leary waited a minute while the rest of the gang got aboard the car and trailer. "Randy, me lad," he said, "I'll always stand back o' my men. But I like 'em to be right. This time I know ye done yer level best to flag that hoghead down, so we'll say no more about it."

"Yes, sir," Randy mumbled. "Thanks, an' I—I'll sure try."

The place where they had been working was only a short distance below the path that led up the mountain to the MacDougal farm. Randy waved good-night to the crew and set off up the grade. He felt a little less cocky than he had half an hour earlier. But his respect for old Dan Leary had deepened. "There," he told himself, "is what I call a man!"

Some summer afternoon you will fly in one of the big airlines transport planes across the mountains of Pennsylvania. League after league you will look down on a green sea of forest, its wave-crests the long, rolling ridges of the hills. Between them are slim, bright ribbons where the rivers run through shadowy valleys, fighting their age-long battle to reach the sea. And following the streams, tunneling the cliffs, bucking the high passes, run darker ribbons—the smoky, man-made pathways of the rails.

IV

Randy sometimes wondered what it would be like to lie abed on the Sunday mornings when he didn't have to work. Mike Hubka often bragged about snoozing till ten o'clock or even noon on those days of rest.

It was different at the MacDougals'. The head of the family held seniority on the engineers' call-board, so he rarely had to take a locomotive out on the Sabbath. But he was a strict Presbyterian and allowed nothing to interfere with churchgoing. Randy was up at six to do the milking, turn the cow out to pasture, feed the chickens, clean out the barn and get washed up for breakfast. After that the family got into its best clothes, ready to start for the ten o'clock service.

This particular Sunday morning Randy was eager for church to be over. He had a plan for the rest of the day. After his second helping of pancakes he broached the subject at breakfast.

"Anybody want to go up on Big Calico with me today?" he asked. "I haven't had a day's exploring since dogwood time, an' it ought to be mighty pretty up there now. How about you, Dad?"

Big Ross shook his head. "My legs aren't as limber as they used to be," he told his son. "I'd only hold ye back. But Jeannie might like to go."

"Jeannie's expecting company later," Mrs. MacDougal put in, "an' you men are not to interfere."

Jeannie's cheeks were red and she kept her eyes on her plate. Randy guessed that a sailor home on shore leave might have something to do with it, but his temptation to tease her was checked by a warning glance from his mother.

"All right," he said, not too regretfully. "I guess I'll just take Babe then. And we'll start right after church, so I won't be here for dinner."

The air was clear and cool when they drove back into the yard at eleven-thirty. Randy stopped to give the big Irish setter a pat. "You know where we're going, Babe?" he asked her. "Up the mountain—yep, that's right—just as soon as I get out o' these clothes!"

When he raced downstairs, three minutes later, his mother handed him a paper bag. "I put up a wee lunch for ye," she said. "Watch out for rattlesnakes an' be sure to come home before dark."

Randy laughed. He had been going up the mountain alone since he was ten years old, and her admonition had never failed to be the same.

Babe bounded ahead of him, her lean, red sides glinting in the sun, and her feathery tail whipping like a flag. She was a perfect companion for a hard day's hiking—tireless, obedient, never too talkative.

They left the clearing by a half-hidden trail that crossed the pasture fence above the barn, and plunged at once into the cool dusk of the woods. The tangle of greenbrier underfoot did not slow Randy's pace. He had on heavy hunting boots and a pair of tough old dungaree trousers—sensible dress for a country where not only rocks and thorny vines but rattlers and copperheads were to be encountered.

Years ago he had blazed this trail, and the weathered marks of his ax were still visible at intervals on the tree trunks. Now he barely noticed them. Long familiarity with the mountainside had taught him short cuts that he used instinctively. The red setter ranged ahead, going six yards to his one, nosing the ground and the thickets for enticing bird smells. Twice, as they climbed through a belt of hemlocks, she came to a firm point—forefoot poised, nose and tail in rigid alignment. Stealing up behind her Randy would clap his hands suddenly and hear the loud whir of wings, as ruffed grouse lifted in bullet-like flight.

There were other live things moving around them in the woods. Squirrels dodged up the tree trunks to safe vantage points above, then jerked their bushy tails and chattered curses at the intruders. Woodpeckers interrupted their tap-tapping to peer down at them. And once a groundhog dove heavily for his burrow with a thud and a rattle of gravel.

On his last visit, back in May, Randy had seen the late mountain dogwood in bloom, lying in a white blanket over half the hillside. Now the snowy blossoms were gone and the foliage of the hardwoods had filled out, thick and green.

The way up was not easy. There were perpendicular ledges and tangles of fallen trees where the boy had to de-tour. But he kept up the steady ascent and in an hour he was a good thousand feet above the level of the farmhouse. He looked around for an opening between the trees that would give him a view of the country below. Soon he came to such a place. A big hemlock had been uprooted by wind and rain and its falling weight had slashed a gap a dozen yards wide. Randy pulled himself up on the rough trunk and sat looking off to the southeast. Below him was the winding valley of the Blacksnake River and part of the big railroad curve. Beyond, to the east, lay the houses and shops of Gaptown, sprawling and ugly in the green folds of the

Alleghenies. And far off to the south rose other ranges, disappearing in a blue haze on the horizon.

Just behind him the boy heard Babe bark once, short and sharp. It was the dog's signal that she had found something. He scrambled to the ground and went up the hill, past the huge mass of earth that clung to the fallen hemlock's base. Where it had been wrenched loose there was a deep hollow in the mountainside, partially sheltered by the overhanging roots and soil.

Babe raced to meet him, then hurried back to sniff at something in the middle of the hollow. Looking more closely Randy saw a dark patch of ashes, four or five half-burned match-sticks, and several cigarette butts. He stood still and tried to reconstruct what had happened here.

There were two layers of ashes. The bottom ones had been washed by rain, while others, evidently more recent, were still dusty gray. A couple of sticks, lying close by, looked as if they had been braced over the fire to boil a kettle. And all around the ashes there were partly obliterated footprints. It was these that Randy studied longest. It seemed to him that some effort had been made to brush them out, but by diligent searching he discovered two that had been made by different sized shoes. One was long and narrow, with a sharp toe. The other, wide and stubby, looked like the mark of an Army boot.

Quickly the boy turned and began casting about in widening circles. This was the kind of problem his woodsman's brain enjoyed. He knew now that at least two men had been here, that they had sat around a campfire and smoked, and probably cooked a meal. He also knew that they had built fires both before and after the heavy shower on Friday afternoon. But who they might be, and what business they had on the mountain, were matters still hidden from him.

After ten minutes of hunting he picked up only two other clues. One was a flattened meat tin of a popular brand. It had been tossed into a crevice deep under the roots of the fallen tree. The other he happened on by the merest chance. It was a two-inch bit of copper wire, half buried in dirt and leaves a few yards from the ashes. Randy puzzled over its significance for a moment, then put it in the pocket of his dungarees.

Further search yielded nothing else of interest and the boy soon left the place to climb higher up the slope. He was close to the crest of the mountain now. Through the trees ahead he could see blue sky to the west. Babe knew they had nearly reached their goal and she raced ahead to wait for her master at the summit. When he overtook her they both sat down to rest and look off across the ridges.

There was no level space on the top of Big Calico. The woods ran up to a sharp, razorback ridge and down the opposite side. But at the point where the boy and his dog had crossed, there was a break in the leaves and a fine view of the next valley. This was one of Randy's favorite haunts. Up here he felt completely cut off from the rest of the world—ruler of a private kingdom so wild and inaccessible that it could never be invaded.

The valley below lay straight as a furrow between the towering ridges. He could see perhaps twenty miles in either direction, and except for a few farms and a village or two along the stream that meandered through it, all that prospect was wooded. There was a break in the farther ridge where the afternoon sun glinted on rails. That was the Ramsville grade. And on the valley floor there were occasional white stretches of road.

Down there, Randy knew, was a community living a separate life of its own. The railroad was the only connecting link in many miles, for no highway crossed the mountain. People in that valley had their own schools and stores and churches. Their contact with other towns lay north-

47

east and southwest, following the river. And what went on over the ridge, in the next valley, was as remote from them as China—even though it might be a scant five miles away.

He was stroking the setter's auburn back as he sat there thinking. Now she quivered a little under his hand and a low rumble came from her throat.

"Quiet, girl," he whispered. "What is it? What do you see?"

Babe got to her feet, still growling faintly. She was looking down the steep slope to the west. After a moment Randy saw something move down there in the thicket. There was a figure climbing toward him. He sat still and gripped the setter's collar, resentful of the intrusion.

Then there was a brown face grinning up at him and a friendly voice said "Hi!" A wiry boy a little younger than himself came bounding up the rough hillside and stopped a few paces below.

"Hi!" Randy returned the greeting. For a few seconds they stared at each other. The newcomer was tanned as dark as an Indian under his tangled thatch of tow-colored hair. He wore a ragged shirt and torn overalls, rolled up above his bare feet.

"That's sure a han'some dog you got." The strange youngster smiled. "Irish setter, ain't it?"

Randy nodded. "You come from down there?" he asked. "What's your name?"

"Yeah, I live in Doran," replied the boy. "Name's Stan Lukowski. What's yours?"

"Randy MacDougal. We've got a farm down the mountain, about halfway to Gaptown. Doran's a coal town, isn't it?"

"That's right. My dad's a miner. Maybe I will be some day, but I like to run the hills best."

"Do you always go barefoot like that?" Randy asked with respect.

"All but in the winter I do. Shoes ain't comfortable for goin' fast an' climbin' trees. My feet's tough. Look."

He drew nearer and held up a blackened sole that looked as hard as a horse's hoof.

"Gosh!" said Randy, impressed. "Aren't you afraid o' snakes, though?"

"Nah—they don't bother me. I'm movin' too fast, mostly. You been up here before, ain't you? I seen your tracks, an' the dog's."

"This is the first time I've been up in a couple o' months. I guess you're on the mountain oftener than that."

"Oh, sure—every day, pretty near. Some days I fish, but this is more fun."

Randy hesitated, then asked the question that had been on the tip of his tongue. "Have you seen any other people up here lately?"

The young woods-runner studied him from under the hanging thatch of his blond hair. "You look all right to me," he said, at length, "so I'll tell you. There's soldiers, o' course. Every once in a while I see 'em scoutin' around, but I never let 'em see me. They don't want anybody up here close to the Gap."

He paused and peered at Randy again. "Day before yesterday I seen somebody else. Two guys. They had a fire goin' under the roots of a tree that blew down—over on your side. I smelled the smoke an' went to see if they had somethin' to eat. They got tough an' chased me out."

Randy nodded. "I saw where their fire had been. What did they look like? They weren't soldiers, were they?"

"Nope. Looked like maybe draft dodgers, or guys hidin' out from the cops. An' I don't think they were just hoboes. Their shoes an' clo'es was too good. One was a tall, skinny guy with light hair, an' the other was short an' heavy-set, sort o' dark."

"They didn't have any guns, I s'pose?" Randy put in.

"Not that I saw. Might ha' been packin' revolvers, though. Only thing they had was a big canvas sack with straps on it, like a back-pack. That was settin' between 'em an' I guess they took their grub out of it."

Stan's eye had strayed to the paper bag by Randy's knee. The older boy grinned and reached for it. "I'm sort of hungry," he said. "How about you?"

They squatted together and shared the "wee lunch" that Mrs. MacDougal had put up. As Randy had expected there was enough for two, and a few scraps were left over for Babe.

All Stan's reserve was gone now. He chatted on like a bluejay, telling of his many experiences on the mountain. He knew how to move quietly, and how to stand motionless for hours when it was necessary. That, he told Randy, was how he found out so many things about animals. He had tracked deer to their sleeping places in the dense hemlock thickets, and he had seen that rarest of woodland sights—a mother fox playing with her kits in front of a carefully hidden den.

"I bet I been over about every inch o' this mountain," he said, and he did not sound boastful. "There's things up here most folks never heard of. You've been around Big Calico plenty, but you never come across a house on top o' the mountain, did you?"

"No," said Randy.

"Well, there is one. An ol' shack that must ha' been built before we was born. The trees are all over an' 'round it now, so it's hard to find, but it sets in a hollow right close to the hogback, over yonder."

"Let's go have a look," Randy suggested. But the other boy shook his head.

"Mm-mm," he said uneasily. "I don't like that place. It's —it's ha'nted or somep'n. Anyhow, I got to go back."

"Oh, well," Randy laughed. "Maybe I'll find it myself some time. I hope I'll be seeing you again. Do you know any o' the railroad men? Ever hop freights over the Gap?"

Stan, it seemed, had a speaking acquaintance with Joe Roan, the freight brakeman.

"If you ever need me or want to see me," Randy told him, "just pass the word by Joe. He knows where I'm working, down there on the line. Better keep an eye out for those two birds that built the fire. They sound like bad medicine to me. So long, Stan."

"So long," called the towhead, waving an arm as he sped

barefoot down the rugged hillside. In a flash he was out of sight and Randy and Babe turned to resume their ramble.

They went south along the ridge for half a mile, while Randy looked in vain for the old shack the Polish boy had described. Then they returned and made a long sweep northward, cutting back as the sun began to sink, and scrambled down the mountain by a different route.

It was suppertime when they reached the clearing and saw the old cow standing by the bars, waiting patiently to be milked.

The pulsing heart of the railroad is the switch-yard. When a long, mixed freight rolls in at the end of a thousand-mile run, it is here that the cars are broken up, spotted on a score of tracks, coupled into fresh trains and sped on their way. Watch an experienced switchman at work on the "hump"—his deft hand-signals and split-second timing—his perfect teamwork with the crew of the switching engine. You will understand why American freight schedules today are the fastest in the history of railroading.

V

Through most of the week that followed, the section gang was working close to Gaptown. There was a lot of ballast-packing to be done at the head of the yard, where the lead tracks branched off to the various spotting locations. Most of the freight that came through the Gap was in solid blocks, headed for the seaboard terminals. But the town was a minor junction point with lines that ran to the north and south, and there was enough switching to keep two tough little "yard-goats" puffing busily.

With most of the tracks in constant use, the gang's work was frequently stopped and Dan Leary had to stay on the alert every minute. Randy didn't mind the interruptions. He liked to stand by and study the skill of the switchers at their task.

There was one old fellow with a gimpy leg who nevertheless seemed to get around as lightly as a boy. He was always at the right place at the right time, and the hand motions with which he signaled the engineer were performed with the grace of an orchestra leader.

At noon on Monday Randy saw the elderly switchman

eating his lunch beside the track and went over to sit beside him. "You're Kim Brawley, aren't you?" the boy asked. "I reckon you know my dad—Ross MacDougal, the hogger. I've heard him tell about you."

"Hm." The old man eyed him. "You must be his youngest boy. Seems to me I rec'lect a couple of others."

"That's right. Bob an' Jim are my brothers. Both railroading overseas with the Army. I've been watching you all morning an' it's quite a sight the way you handle those cars."

"Well, it ain't difficult after you been at it long as I have. Forty years I've worked the yard—an' most o' the time for this road."

"Gosh," said Randy, "you must remember the old days before automatic couplers!"

Brawley laughed. "I don't go quite that far back. 'Twas late in the eighties that they come in. But the fellers that taught me was all pin-couplin' men. Most of 'em had fingers gone. They used to have a sayin' there was only two kinds o' switchmen—the quick an' the dead. That was when they had to run along between the cars an' wait for just the right second to pull the pin.

"There was worse things than that about switchin' in the old times, though. None o' the switch-frogs had wood between like they do now. You had to watch your step or you'd get a foot caught just when a car was comin' down the line. That happened to me once. I jerked her out by main strength an' busted my ankle so it's bothered me ever since. But that was a heap sight better'n losin' the foot!"

Randy munched a sandwich and stared out at the yard. "How can you tell just how fast to let a car come off the hump?" he asked. "They always seem to slide down easy an' come up to their string just hard enough to close the coupling."

"It's one o' the tricks you learn," said the old man. "Have to know somethin' about the force o' gravity. You need to watch it, though. A heavy car's got a lot more roll than a light one. I've seen greenhorns smack a string so hard they drifted half the length o' the yard."

He tossed away the butt of the stogie he had been smoking and got spryly to his feet. "Well, kid," he said, "you stick to railroadin', but don't follow my trail. No future in switchin'. I'll be wavin' signals to you in your cab one o' these days." Then with a grin he limped back to his job.

The new man, Burns, had been on hand with the rest of the gang that morning. His blistered palms were taped with adhesive bandage and he wore a blue work-shirt. "I'm going to stick to this till I'm earning my pay, at least," he told Randy.

As the days passed the boy could see that he was really trying. His efforts were clumsy and it was quite evident that he had never done heavy manual work before, but he was no quitter. There was one thing about him that Randy could not understand. Whenever a train came down the grade, Burns watched it as if fascinated. Even though it was several tracks away and did not interfere with the ballast work, the man would stand with his shovel poised and stare at the passing cars. Once or twice Dan Leary spoke to him sharply on such occasions and he jumped back to work with a sheepish grin.

"I always liked to watch trains, even when I was a kid," he told Randy. "But I've never had much chance to do it till now."

The high iron was humming with traffic that week. There were extras every few minutes, it seemed to the boy. Trains of flat-cars loaded with anti-aircraft guns and jeeps and huge radial bomber engines shrouded under canvas covers; packed troop trains and their accompanying motorized equipment; and always, night and day, the long hauls of coal gondolas and oil tankers.

Sometimes, while they waited for a train to pass, Randy saw Burns pull out that little red notebook and write something in it.

"You use that book plenty," he laughed once. "Going to buy another shirt?"

Behind the thick lenses of his spectacles, the novice section hand looked up quickly. "No, not this time," he replied. "I've just made a habit of jotting down my thoughts. I—I used to be a poet, you see. Not that it's anything to be ashamed of."

"Gosh, no!" Randy answered. "I'd be mighty proud if I could write poetry an' things. You must have a real education. Did you go to college?"

"Yes." Burns nodded as he went back to work. He seemed to prefer to let the conversation die there, and it was not until a day or two later that Randy found a chance to learn more about him.

They were sitting on a bench in the shade of the section house eating their lunch.

"Mighty hot, isn't it?" said Randy. "You seem to stand it a lot better'n you did that first day, though."

"I've been in some very hot places," Burns told him. "The Venezuela jungle, for instance, and the Arizona desert. This climate is really comfortable."

The boy's eyes opened wider. "Gee," he said, "for a bookkeeper you've certainly been around. When were you in Venezuela?"

"Seven or eight years ago," Burns replied with his vague smile. "The winter of thirty-six, I think it was. I've always wanted to see strange places and, being single, there was nothing to keep me home. I went down there for one of the big oil companies, working in the office. There was too much malaria around to suit me so I quit after a few months."

"What other places have you been?" Randy asked eagerly.

"Well, I spent two years in Honolulu when I was young, and I've lived in quite a few of the western states."

"Ever go to Europe? Scotland, maybe?"

Burns laughed. "Not to Scotland. But Europe, yes. I was assistant purser on a small liner to the Mediterranean for several voyages."

Randy felt a growing respect for this queer section hand. But the more he thought about it the stranger it seemed that a well-educated man—a poet and world-traveler—should have come down to such a humdrum job. Perhaps drink was his trouble. Yet the boy had never noticed the smell of liquor on his breath when he was working with the gang. Or it might have been an underlying streak of restlessness. In any case the fellow's character was a puzzle Randy gave up trying to solve.

There was a light drizzle of rain all day Thursday, and firemen on the upbound trains had to work the sand as they tackled the grade. The section crew labored in wet clothes, their spirits kept up only by old Dan's unquenchable good humor. "Wait till the next hot day, b'ys," he would tell them. "Ye'll be wishin' then for some o' this refreshin' moisture. Better enj'y it while it lasts!"

By Friday morning a chilly wind from the north had swept the rain away and there was blue sky between the racing clouds overhead. It was a brisk day—a day for hard work. When he reached the section house Randy saw the rail-car and trailer out on the siding.

"We'll be goin' up the grade today," Leary announced. "There's a culvert needs cleanin' out, an' some rock fell in the cut last night. The sooner we're on our way, the quicker ye can warm up on the job!"

For several miles along the side of the big curve, the four-track road had been cut out of the solid rock of the mountain. There were sheer cliffs rising four or five hundred feet in many places. After rains it was not uncommon for small pieces of the rock face to loosen and drop off. Occasionally a fragment fell on the track itself or even on top of a train, but for the most part the only damage done by rock slides was to block the broad ditch at the side of the right-of-way.

That was what the gang found when they piled off the trailer on the sidetrack, halfway up the grade. Two or three tons of crumbling stone had tumbled from somewhere on the blast-scarred face of the cliff and lay in an ugly heap in the ditch. Randy and half a dozen other members of the crew were told off to clear the rubble away. Old Dan took the rest up the track to work in the culvert.

There was no easy way to move the rock. It was a matter of breaking up the large boulders, picking them up and carrying them to the bank above the ditch. Burns had his coat on when he started work, but after fifteen minutes of toil on the rock-pile he was glad to take it off and lay it on the bank.

"Whew!" He smiled at Randy. "I thought it was a cold morning until now."

The boy was sweating over a slab of stone a yard across. "Come on and give me a hand with this," he said. "It isn't so heavy—just awkward to lift."

Between them they got the rock off the ground and hoisted it into place in the neat row above the ditch. A train came rumbling past down the grade at that moment, drowning out all other sounds. It was sheer luck that made Randy look up as he wiped his forehead on his sleeve. What he saw sent him into frenzied action. He grabbed his companion's arm and jerked him toward the track, almost falling as he scrambled up the ballast. Where they had stood only two seconds before, a piece of rock as big as a barrel crashed into the ditch.

Randy was breathless and shaking. His heart felt like a cold lump somewhere in the neighborhood of his throat, for he knew he had never been so close to death before.

The other track workers, farther up the ditch, were unhurt. But they stood with their mouths hanging open in fright. Only Burns seemed unmoved. He patted Randy gently on the back and grinned in his vague way. "That was a pretty close shave, wasn't it?" he said with a shake of his head.

Old Dan Leary had seen the rock fall, and he came galloping down the track at top speed. "Jeepers!" he panted, his brogue thickening as always in excitement. "I should ha' stuck wid yez! When there's a slide the rocks sometimes

keep on fallin'. 'Twas lucky ye weren't hit, b'ys!"

He stood by while the rest of the rock was cleared from the ditch, watching the cliff like a hawk. Randy had a squeamish feeling about going back to the job. But he refused to admit he had less courage than Burns, who was working as calmly as if nothing had happened.

By noon they had piled all the stone along the bank. Randy saw Burns pick up his coat and brush off some scraps of mud and rock that had spattered it. "Not very clean work," the man smiled, "but I enjoy it more than I expected."

They went on up the track to the rail-car and got their lunches. Mike Hubka was still excited. He had seen the rock fall from where he was working, and now he had a lot of questions to ask.

"Gee!" he told Randy. "You sure moved fast! Looked to me like you saved that guy's life. I bet he was scared!"

"That was the funny part of it," Randy replied. "He just laughed, cool as a cucumber, an' told me it was a close shave. I never thought he had it in him."

That afternoon they all worked on the culvert and packed ballast higher up the grade. When quitting time came, everybody except Randy got aboard the car and trailer and chugged off toward Gaptown. The boy walked along the embankment in the same direction, headed for the hill path that would take him home. As he passed the scene of the rock slide he stopped to look at the place again. Down in the ditch, half-concealed by a bit of loose stone, something red caught his eye. It was Burns' notebook, and he figured it must have fallen from the man's pocket when he laid his coat aside.

Randy jumped down into the ditch and picked it up. He wondered if Burns might need it that night. He could jump a down freight and get to town about as soon as the rest of the gang. And Jean would give him a ride home in the car.

There was a train easing down around the curve now, so he waited, idly turning the pages of the little book. To his surprise there were no words or sentences written in it. Instead each page bore a date and a series of meaningless figures and letters. He thrust the notebook into his overalls pocket, waited till the engine and tender rumbled by and made his sprint for the ladder of a passing boxcar. A moment later he was riding the roof toward town.

Clustered close to roundhouse and yards, in every junction town and division point, are the railroad boarding-houses. They are run by decent, motherly women, good cooks for the most part, many of them widows of old-time railroaders. At any hour of day or night they are ready with food and hot coffee for the men who come in off their runs, hungry and tired. And they know how to give comfort and sound advice to homesick youngsters making their start on the iron trail.

VI

Randy waited till the through freight reached the lower end of the yard before he dropped off. A shabby street ran along beside the tracks, and the boy saw one of the older men from the section gang walking down it.

"Did you see where Burns went?" Randy asked him.

"Burns? Oh, that new feller? Nope. He was ahead o' me. I know where he hangs out, though. Over to Mrs. Ryan's, on Third Street. You'll likely find him there, kid."

Randy thanked him and turned the corner, heading southward. A two-block walk past dingy old dwellings, small stores and a saloon or two brought him to a brown-painted, three-story house with a sign in the window: "Mrs. P. J. Ryan, Board and Rooms."

Through the screen door came the odor of boiling cabbage. He knocked, and a loud, cheery voice called, "Come in!"

Mrs. Ryan appeared in the kitchen door, wiping her hands on her apron. She was a stout, gray-haired woman with a quick smile.

"You looking for a room, son?" she asked. "Oh—I see

69

who y' are now. Big Ross MacDougal's boy, ain't you? My Pat used to fire for your dad back in the old days. Come in an' have a cup o' coffee."

"Thanks just the same," Randy told her, "but I can't stop. I was looking for one o' your boarders—Mr. Burns."

The smile left her face. "I don't know whether you could call him one o' my boarders," she said. "He's a queer one. I'm used to odd hours, but you'd think a section hand would sleep nights. Sometimes he's here an' sometimes not. He don't act like a hard drinker, but he's liable to be out till two or three o'clock in the mornin', or not come in at all. I don't like such goin's-on."

"He hasn't been in since he quit at four o'clock?" the boy asked. "Oh, well, I'll see him on the job tomorrow. I've got to catch my sister before she starts home in the car. Good-night, Mrs. Ryan."

The notebook was still in his pocket as he went down the street. He could have left it with the boarding-house keeper, but she was obviously none too fond of Burns. He decided to wait and return it to its owner in the morning.

The huge Gaptown car-shops, where half the rolling-stock of the railroad was built or repaired, stretched for nearly a mile along the tracks. The offices, where Jeannie worked, were at the farther end, close to the center of town. It would take less time to reach the roundhouse, and Randy knew the girl would stop there to pick up his father. He trotted a few blocks and crossed the tracks to the smoke-blackened building.

Nearly a dozen locomotives were on the stall tracks that radiated from the turntable. They loomed gigantic in the half darkness. The newly arrived engines breathed and panted like enormous beasts and there was a clank of grates as the hot ashes were dropped into steaming pits below. Randy breathed the smoky air with delight. Ever since he had been big enough to walk, the roundhouse had fascinated him.

His father and a couple of other hoggers were back in the washroom, scrubbing the grease off their hands and swapping yarns.

"Yep," old Eddie Smith was saying, "the airbrake is sure a great thing. Them runaways just don't happen no more."

Bill Anson, youngest of the trio, nodded to Randy. "Eddie," he said, "speakin' o' runaways, that one you had in Mexico was a honey. I bet young Mac here never heard about it. Why don't you tell him?"

"Oh, that," replied the old engineer indifferently. "Yeah,

that was quite a picnic. Don't reckon the kid would be much interested though."

"Gee," Randy put in, "o' course I would!"

"Well," said Eddie, sputtering as he splashed water over his head, "it was forty year ago, on a branch line in the Sonora mountains. The Mexicans was backward about improvements—still used hand-broke, pin-coupled freight cars, an' the engines was held together with solder. This trip we was haulin' fifteen cars o' silver down to the coast. The load was worth a million bucks, more or less, an' the mine manager was ridin' the cab, scared we'd be held up by bandits. It was gittin' dark an' a storm was comin' up, too. This fool manager was plumb loco—kep' tellin' me we had to go faster. The grade was 'round three-an'-a-half per cent an' the road was all curves, huggin' the side of a cliff.

"Well, I was young an' crazy an' I let her rip. We must ha' been hittin' fifty an hour. 'Bout then my ashcat looked back an' yelled that we'd lost two cars an' the caboose. The head-end brakie crawled in over the tender an' told us his brakes wouldn't hold. We was really runnin' wild. 'Course there was nothin' to do but throw the Johnson bar in the corner—full reverse. An' would you believe it, right that minute, with the wheels screamin' on the rails, an' the heavy cars tryin' to climb up our back, I seen the trestle was gone, a hundred yards ahead. Boy, that was a nasty sight! We couldn't jump, 'cause there was nothin' below but a thousand-foot canyon. Yep, we was in a jam that time."

"Gosh!" breathed Randy. "Wh-what happened to you?"

"Killed," said Smith calmly. "All of us killed dead."

At that Anson burst into a guffaw and slapped his thigh. "Ho—ho—ho!" he roared. "Every time you tell it, it gets better, Eddie. I'm s'prised you took in young Mac, though. You'd think he'd ha' heard the yarn from Big Ross."

Ross MacDougal stretched his massive arms and yawned. "No," he said, "when I tell it, it took place in the Hielands o' Scotland. But I dinna trouble my family wi' such foolishness."

Randy was already over his embarrassment and busily memorizing the story so that he could pass it on to Mike Hubka. But at that moment an auto horn honked outside, and he followed his father to the little parking place behind the engine house. Jean was waiting there in the car.

On the way home he described the rock fall, but he was careful not to mention how close he had come to being hit. He knew his mother would worry if she heard the tale, and having a railroad family was bad enough for her as it was.

Randy had done the chores and eaten supper before he thought of the notebook again. He went out to the grape arbor, where there was still light enough for reading, and took the little book out of his pocket. For a moment he had a guilty feeling. Perhaps he had no right to pry into another man's secrets. But when Burns had told him he was a writer, Randy's interest had been aroused. He was curious to see how ideas took shape on paper, and surely there was no harm in seeing for himself when he had such an opportunity.

Once more he leafed through all the pages, looking for lines of verse or scraps of prose. There was nothing of the kind to be found—not even the reminder to buy a workshirt.

The dates at the top of each page started about two weeks before, and the last one was today's. The entries below seemed to be in a sort of code. They were arranged in neat columns, sometimes thirty or forty to a page, and each symbol was made up of one or more letters and a figure. Occasionally one of them was underlined. A typical series of entries read like this: "MF55, OT61, C70, C63, MF52, TP15, C80, MF70, TP12, TP14, OT78, G&T54," etc.

For ten minutes Randy puzzled over the jottings and

made neither head nor tail of them. Then a half-remembered conversation flashed through his mind. Something about troop trains—how many men a car would hold. He recalled the fixed expression on Burns' face as he watched the passing cars, and how he reached for notebook and pencil when the last one rolled by. That day—the boy looked again at the date on the page—there had been three troop trains fairly close together. Fifteen cars in the first one, he remembered, and two more, half an hour later—one with twelve cars and the other with fourteen. He had it now—the key to everything written in the book!

Those underlined symbols seemed to jump out at him from the page. "TP15 . . . TP12, TP14." The letters "TP" must stand for "troop," or possibly "troop passenger." With that clue he quickly figured out the rest. "MF" was probably "mixed freight." "OT" might be "oil tanks." "C" for "coal," and so on. "G&T54" stopped him for a minute. Then he recalled a string of flatcars loaded with guns and tanks that had gone through that same day. Burns had made a complete record of all the eastbound freight and troop movements over the main line!

The discovery hit Randy like an electric shock. He tried to think of some innocent reason why a section hand would keep such a list. There was none. Now that he knew Burns had lied to him about what was written in the book, the facts appeared blacker every moment. Information like that would be dangerous in the wrong hands, and in his heart the boy no longer doubted that it had been collected for just such a purpose.

What was he going to do about it? He hesitated to tell his father, for he had a feeling that the hard-headed Scot would laugh at his suspicions. Yet somebody in authority ought to be given a chance to investigate.

Randy took Babe for a short run through the pasture in the twilight, then went to bed. It was a cool night, ideal weather for sleeping, but he lay awake worrying for an hour or more. At last he decided to talk to Joe Roan if he could find him. The brakeman knew some of the railroad detectives and could advise Randy on how to proceed.

In the morning the boy left the house early and hurried down to the tracks. He went up along the curve to the spot where the rock slide had taken place and left the little red notebook just as he had found it. Then he hopped an eastbound freight as usual and reported for work at the section house.

Dan Leary was fuming. "Short-handed again!" he roared

as he counted up the crew. "That pasty-faced Burns has quit on us—got his time this mornin'."

Randy, who had been wondering if he could act naturally when he met Burns again, heard this announcement with mixed feelings. In a way he was relieved. But the fact that the man had drawn his pay and quit after missing the book seemed to prove more strongly than ever that he was a spy.

The gang went up the line to work. At lunch-time Randy took a few minutes to return to the rock slide. The notebook lay there undisturbed, and he picked it up and put it in his pocket. All afternoon he watched the passing freights and shortly before quitting-time he saw Joe Roan waving to him from a down-bound caboose. That meant the brakeman was finishing his run from the west. He would be in Gaptown that night.

At four o'clock Randy rode down to the yard with the rest of the crew and made a bee-line for town. He knew where his friend lived. Roan was a bachelor and had a room at Ma Peterson's boarding-house. There were a couple of switchmen sitting in rockers on the porch when he arrived, and one of them called up the stairs to tell Joe he had company.

"Come on up, kid," said the brakeman. "I'm just gettin'

77

my clothes off to take a shower. What's new?"

Randy went into the clean little room and sat down on the narrow bed. Joe was stripped to the waist. He was a well-muscled young man of twenty-five—an ex-Navy man, discharged after Pearl Harbor, where he had lost the sight of one eye.

"You look worried, Randy," the brakeman joked. "What you got—girl trouble? If so, you've come to the right place."

Randy shook his head. "I'm afraid it's worse'n that," he answered. "What would you think if you knew a strange section hand was keeping secret notes of all the troop trains and war freight going east through the Gap?"

Roan frowned. "I'd sock him on the whiskers first an' ask questions afterward," he said with vehemence. "I'd say to myself, 'That guy's gettin' his pay checks in German marks,' an' I wouldn't fool around."

"All right," said Randy. "Look at this." And he held out the little red notebook.

In the next five minutes he told his friend all that he knew about Burns and the daily notations in the book. "And now," he concluded, "the fellow's quit his job. I'm afraid he's skipped out for good."

There was a gleam in Roan's good eye. "I've got to take

a bath an' get dressed," he said. "But I don't think you ought to wait. Here, I'll write a note for you to take to Ben Small. He's that road dick I was tellin' you about an' he'll know what to do. I reckon you'll find him over at the Allegheny House. That's where he stays when he's in town."

Roan pulled a piece of paper out of the table drawer and scribbled a few words on it. "That'll tell him you're all right an' a friend o' mine," he said. "Now you'd better get goin'. An' let me know what happens. Looks to me like this is really the goods!"

On a hot night in July you can lie out in an Iowa field and hear the corn grow. You can hear the creak and rustle and push of a million husky stalks shooting upward whole inches between sunset and sunrise. Soaking rain, blazing sun and rich, black prairie soil combine to make America's corn-belt the greatest food-producing area on earth; the giant bread-basket of the nation. Out of it, night and day, roll the trainloads of corn and pork and beef to feed a hungry world.

VII

The Allegheny House was on the principal business street of the city, two blocks from the station. It was an old-fashioned commercial hotel, catering to traveling salesmen from the wholesale houses. Randy had never visited it before but he knew the grimy five-story brick building well by sight. A dozen men were sitting around the lobby on worn plush chairs, smoking, reading newspapers or exchanging stories. Most of them were in their shirt-sleeves, for it was a hot evening.

A bored-looking clerk stood behind the desk picking his teeth and making an occasional languid gesture with a fly-swatter. He paid no attention to Randy at first, and the boy had to repeat his question.

"Look," he said. "Can't you tell me if Mr. Small is here? I've got to see him and it's important."

"Mr. Small is not in," the clerk replied coldly. "I don't keep informed of his movements but you might find him here tomorrow or next day. If you have a message you can leave it and I'll put it in his box."

Randy was disappointed, but there was no more he could do. He read the note Roan had written. It said:

"This is to interduse Randy McDugle. His father is a R.R. man and he is O.K. He has got some dope will interst you.

"JOE ROAN."

Randy borrowed the clerk's pen and wrote beneath:

"I will come back tomorrow (Sunday) after church.

"RANDALL MACDOUGAL."

When he had seen the message placed in a mail-box behind the desk, he left the hotel and started for home. Jeannie's work was over at noon on Saturday, so he would have to pick up a ride on a freight if he could. He took a side street, heading over toward the tracks and soon found himself passing Ma Peterson's boarding-house once more. Joe Roan was just coming down the steps, dressed in clean clothes, his hair carefully parted and groomed.

"What's the matter, kid?" he asked. "Couldn't you find him?"

"No. I guess he won't be back before tomorrow. I'll try again then."

Roan walked on with him down the street. "I just remembered somethin'," he said. "Glad you came back this way, because I wanted to tell you. I was goin' up the grade on a freight, 'bout the time it got dark last night. Along there where the slide was I happened to look down an' saw a man movin' in the right-hand ditch. He was stooped over like he was huntin' for somethin'."

"What sort of man?" asked Randy quickly. "Could you tell how he looked?"

"No—too dark. But I'd say he was sort o' heavy-set. Had a coat an' hat on."

"That sounds like Burns," said the boy. "I had a hunch he might have gone back there, soon as he found he didn't have the book. An' when he couldn't locate it, he got scared. That would explain why he quit this morning."

"Right." Roan nodded. "Say—er—you know, Randy, if you're headin' home I might go along with you. That's a mighty cute sister o' yours, an' last time I saw her she sort o' hinted she'd be home tonight."

Randy laughed. "You'll probably have competition," he said. "But come ahead. More power to you!"

They were crossing the next street when the boy glanced to his left and stopped in the middle of a stride. A short block away he had seen a man going into a corner saloon.

"Look, Joe!" he gasped. "Did you see that guy? It was Burns—I'm sure of it! Come on—let's get up there!"

They ran the length of the block and walked up to the bar-room door side by side. It was a small, shabby place, with sawdust on the floor and a couple of greasy tables in front. There were three men at the bar and two more sitting at one of the tables. The barkeep wiped a glass and stared at Joe and Randy with a fishy eye.

"He's not here," Randy whispered. "Must have gone on through to the back room."

"You want somep'n, gents?" asked the bartender sourly.

"Yeah. You got a washroom back there?" Roan replied.

The man nodded and jerked a thumb toward a door at the end of the bar. They crossed the floor together and Joe turned the knob. Randy, right behind him, saw that the small room was empty. There was another door at the rear, opening out into the alley, but it was bolted on the inside.

"Guess you must ha' been mistaken, kid," said Roan. "Maybe one o' those birds at the bar looked a little like him, huh?"

"No." Randy shook his head. "None of 'em was the man I saw. He's either hiding somewhere in the building or he got out the back way an' somebody locked that door after him."

He went to the dusty little window and looked down the alley but the only sign of life there was a lean gray cat sniffing at scattered rubbish. "I guess we drew a blank here," he said. "Might as well be on our way."

They went out the way they came in, followed by a scowling look from the bartender.

"Oh, well," said Joe, "you might ha' been mistaken—a block away like that. Anyhow, Ben Small's the man to pick him up if he's still around these parts. You talk to Ben tomorrow."

They were late for supper, but Mrs. MacDougal had a good meal waiting for them. While Jeannie and Joe sat out in the moonlit arbor afterward, Randy did his chores, read awhile and went to bed. He was eager for Sunday to come.

The next morning dawned hot and cloudless. The boy went with his family to church in Gaptown, but the moment the service was over he hurried off to the Allegheny House.

Sunday morning peace reigned in the dingy lobby. The chairs stood empty, and the heat, the buzzing flies and the drowsy clerk had the place to themselves.

"Heh? Ben Small? Yeah, he said he was expectin' you,"

the clerk replied to Randy's inquiry. "You'll find him up in his room—four-eleven."

The old colored man who ran the creaking elevator let Randy off at the fourth floor and a moment later he knocked on the detective's door.

"Come in," said a high-pitched, gentle voice.

The boy entered and found himself in a big corner room with windows open on two sides to let in what breeze might be stirring. Small was sitting in a sturdy rocking-chair, easing his bulk slowly forward and back. He was not very tall but immensely fat—a balloon-shaped man with small, sleepy-looking eyes and a bald head on which tiny beads of perspiration lay like dew. He had a palm-leaf fan in one pudgy hand.

"Mr. Small?" Randy asked. "I'm Randy MacDougal. Guess you got the note I left?"

"That's right. Sit down, young man, and tell me what's on your mind."

"It's about a man named Burns—Lew Burns," Randy began. "He's been working on Dan Leary's section gang the last couple of weeks. Saturday morning he got his time and quit. Didn't come to work.

"He was sort of a queer duck, harmless looking, an' wore

86

thick glasses. Said his eyes were bad. He told me he'd always been a bookkeeper but he'd traveled a lot. His hands were soft an' I guess he never did much hard work before. His story was that he wanted to help in the war, so he took a track job on the railroad.

"Well, I used to see him watching all the trains that went past eastbound. Then every once in a while he'd write something down in a little book he carried. Friday we were clearing up a rock slide an' he took his coat off an' laid it on the bank beside the track. When he picked it up the notebook must have fallen out of his pocket. I found it after he'd gone home an' tried to take it to him but he hadn't been to his boarding-house."

Randy took the red notebook from his pocket and held it out to the detective. "Here it is," he said. "An' I'm pretty sure I know what those numbers mean that are written in it."

Small flipped open the cover with one hand and continued to fan himself with the other. He said nothing for several minutes, while he scanned page after page.

"Well," he said at last, "what's your theory?"

"I remember some of those days," Randy told him, "an' some o' the trains that came down the grade. The way I figure it, those letters stand for the kind of train, an' the numbers tell how many cars were in it. For instance, there were three troop trains pretty close together that first day. They were pulling fifteen, twelve an' fourteen cars apiece. An' right afterward there was a long string o' flats with guns and tanks. All the other letters an' figures check, too—mixed freight, oil tank cars, coal, an' so forth."

"Hm," said Small mildly.

"Burns had been getting along all right," Randy continued. "An' he said he liked his job. But as soon as he lost that book he quit in a hurry. It looks to me as if he got scared."

The detective nodded but made no comment. He was still studying the pages of the notebook.

"I went to Mrs. Ryan's boarding-house looking for him," Randy said. "She didn't seem to like him much. Told me he had queer habits—used to be out late a lot of nights. Yesterday afternoon, after I left here, I thought I saw him go into a saloon, over near the tracks. Joe Roan and I followed him in there but he'd either hid out or gone. He wasn't in sight in the bar."

"Hm," Small said again. "Can you give me a good description of him? Burns sounds like a Scotch or Irish name."

"He's pretty good-sized," Randy replied. "About five-eleven an' weighs maybe a hundred an' eighty-five or ninety. I'd judge he was a little over forty—close to forty-five. Pale complexion, only he got sunburned a couple o' times, out on the job. His hair's sort of grayish-blond an' short. Stands up stiff on top of his head. His eyes are pale blue, an' as I said, he wears thick glasses. When he first came to work, an' again yesterday, he was wearing a dark brown suit an' a brown felt hat. As for his name, he doesn't look like any Scotchman I ever saw—more like a Swede or—or a German."

The boy waited expectantly but Small went on rocking slowly and fanning himself.

At last he heaved his plump body out of the chair and struggled into a seersucker coat that matched his stretched and wrinkled trousers. He took a straw hat off the bureau and perched it on top of his bald head. The red notebook he placed in his inside breast pocket.

"I'd like to keep this a spell," he said with a sigh. "Tell me again where Mrs. Ryan's place is, and also this saloon where you thought Burns went in."

Randy gave him their locations and the fat man nodded. "I'll know where to reach you if I need you," he told the boy. "I think I'll take a walk now."

They went down in the elevator together, and at the door

of the hotel Small said good-by in his little, high voice. Randy watched him stroll off up the street. He moved slowly, like a man with no particular destination in mind and no desire to hurry. And the direction he took was not toward the railroad yards but away from them. The boy was disappointed. This detective seemed to be anything but the man of action he had hoped to meet.

Randy got home in time for dinner at one o'clock and took a short hike with the setter afterward. There was no time for a real trip to the top of the mountain, but they skirted the steeper slopes, walking three or four miles through the woods. The boy wondered what Stan Lukowski was doing. He had half expected the young Pole would come over the mountain to see him before this. On his next day off, he promised himself, he would go up on Big Calico and hunt till he found the old cabin Stan had mentioned. It bothered him to think that a strange youngster from the next valley should know more about the mountain than he did.

He was late with the chores that night and by the time he had finished milking dusk had fallen. He had just picked up the pail and started toward the house when he heard Babe bark suddenly. She was tied up to her kennel near the end of the barn.

Randy ran back to the corner of the building and saw the dog straining at her leash, barking at two figures that moved down across the pasture. In the half light he could make out only that they were men, one of them taller than the other, and that they were hurrying. The tall one looked back at the dog and caught sight of Randy. Then they both broke into a run. A moment later they had been swallowed up by the dense brush beyond the pasture fence.

The boy took his milk down to the cool cellar and went quickly to the hall closet for a flashlight. When he pressed the switch there was only a feeble glow in the bulb, and he remembered that the war had made it difficult to get batteries. He raced back to the shed and lighted an oil lantern.

It took him only a moment to unsnap the leash from Babe's collar. She bounded off like a flash and he ran after her, the lantern swinging at his side. The dog reached the spot where she had first seen the trespassers and nosed eagerly along, following their trail. The ground was hard and dry and covered with short-cropped pasture grass. There was no visible track on the hillside. Randy went down the slope close behind the setter till they reached the fence and the woods. There she would have kept up the pursuit, but he called her back. He had no intention of following the men into the brush.

He was turning to go home when he noticed a swampy spot near the pasture boundary. He bent down, holding the light close to the ground, and saw that there were footprints in the mud—two sets of them—a yard or two apart. One man's shoes had left long, narrow tracks. The other's were broad and blunt-toed. The more he looked at them the surer he became that they were made by the same men who had built the campfire on the mountain.

Babe barked once or twice, then whimpered and looked up at him as he gripped her collar. Everything was quiet in the woods below. Not even the rustle of a leaf broke the stillness. He wondered if the two were watching him from the thicket. Then he laughed at his own imaginings. They were probably just a couple of town lads, afraid of a barking dog.

"Come on, Babe," he said. "Time to go home." And blowing out the lantern he followed the setter up the hill.

Mountain railroading is a never-ending battle against weather. There is bitter winter cold that ices the rails and freezes the switches; blizzards that howl through the gaps and pile the drifts higher than the cab windows; fog that blurs headlamps and hides signal lights; and in summer the fierce, black storms that funnel up the valleys to shake the mountain with their thunderclaps and undermine the tracks with floods of rain.

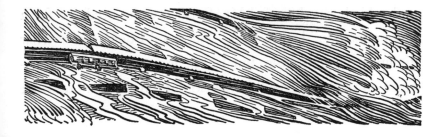

VIII

That Monday morning was oppressively hot and sultry. Big Ross MacDougal frowned over his breakfast coffee.

"It's a weather-breeder," he announced. "No life in the air. That means we'll have a change before night. Better take a raincoat wi' ye, Jeannie lass. And it 'ud be a help if dry clothes were laid out for Randy an' me."

Randy took his time going down to work. It was no morning to hurry. The seven o'clock whistle was blowing as he swung off a freight in the yard, and most of the crew were already assembled by the section house. He was surprised to see a strange figure among them—the unmistakable barrel shape of Ben Small.

The railroad detective was mopping his damp forehead and talking to Dan Leary when the boy came up.

The old section foreman looked sternly at Randy from under his bushy brows. "Mr. Small says he needs ye fer a few hours, b'y," he growled. "Faith, an' I don't know what divilment ye've been in, but I hope it's nothin' to bring disgrace on the gang. We'll be workin' up in the cut. Get back to the job as soon as ye can."

Randy caught the flicker of the big Irishman's eyelid and tried to look properly crestfallen. "Yes, sir," he replied soberly. "I'll be with you just as quick as they let me come."

He walked away in company with the fat detective, and it was not until they were well out of earshot of the group that Small spoke.

"I told him you were helping us with an investigation," he chuckled. "He doesn't know Burns is mixed up in it, but he understands you're not in any trouble yourself. That remark was just for the benefit of the rest of the crew."

"That's what I thought," said Randy. "Did you have any luck finding Burns?"

"Not yet. I tried Mrs. Ryan's and found he'd been back there late Friday night. Packed his suitcase and walked out. Didn't leave any new address, and there were no papers or other clues in his room. He was in McCabe's bar for a beer about ten o'clock Saturday but they hadn't seen him since. That other saloon you mentioned is run by a man named Bronsky. He's a foreigner and a tough customer. Just shut up like a clam when I started to question him. There might be something there, because I'm pretty sure Burns hasn't left town. At least I know he didn't buy a railroad ticket."

Small stopped and puffed and wiped his round, perspiring

face. "Weather like this I'd rather be sitting still," he said plaintively. "But the big jobs always seem to come on hot days. I'm beginning to think this is a big job. That's why I called the F.B.I. last night. They've sent one of their best men—K. P. Harrow—and he's getting in from Pittsburgh this morning. We'll meet him at the hotel."

There was no more conversation until they reached the Allegheny House. Seated in a far corner of the lobby was a man who rose when Small nodded to him and entered the elevator with them. Randy was impressed by his bearing. He was a wiry, athletic man in his late thirties, with the build and the face of a big-league ball player. His red-brown hair was crisp and curly, and his gray eyes missed nothing that went on around him.

When they were inside the detective's room, Small introduced Randy to Harrow and sank, panting, into his rocking-chair.

"Sit down, gentlemen," he urged, "while I get this necktie off."

Harrow grinned, showing a set of strong, even teeth. "It must be something serious," he said, "to make you hustle like this on a hot morning, Mr. Small. Take your time and get comfortable."

The railroad detective loosened his wet shirt collar and put his fan in motion. "Well," he said, "I guess the best way to start is to let the boy tell you his story. Go ahead, son."

Randy faced the Federal man and outlined the facts very much as he had done the day before. When he came to the part about the red notebook, Small produced it and put it in Harrow's hands.

The F.B.I. agent looked from one to the other of them. "Wait a bit," he said. "I suppose two or three people have handled this. And none of you took the trouble to examine it for finger-prints? That's too bad, because we might have got something that way. Okay, go on."

"Gee," said Randy regretfully. "I never thought about that. There might be some prints on the inside pages, though, where it hasn't been pawed over so much."

He went on to describe some of the trains that had passed and pointed out how the figures in the book fitted them as to type and number of cars.

Harrow held the cover in a clean handkerchief and turned the pages carefully with his finger-tips as he studied the daily entries. "What's this number back here by itself on the last page?" he asked.

Randy leaned over and looked. Written very faintly in

pencil, up close to the binding edge, he saw the figures "4-2881."

"I don't know," he said. "Somehow I never noticed that one before."

"You didn't write it, did you, Small?" Harrow asked.

"No. It must have been there all the time, but I didn't pay much attention to the blank pages at the back."

"I think I know what it is," said the F.B.I. man. "We'll check on it in a few minutes. Well, what happened next?"

Randy told about his visit to Mrs. Ryan's and the unsuccessful search at Bronsky's bar. "There's something else I think you ought to know," he said. "Probably it's got no connection with Burns, but let me tell you anyhow."

He gave the Federal man a description of the tracks he had found beside the campfire on the mountain, and the appearance of the two men Stan Lukowski had seen.

"Last night," he continued, "I think I saw that pair. They were running down through our pasture and I found some footprints in the mud. They were the same two fellows, all right. But they'd got away in the woods, heading towards town, and I didn't follow them."

Harrow seemed more interested in these facts than Randy had expected. He made several notes on the back of an envelope and nodded as the boy talked.

"All right," he said, when Randy had finished. "Here's what we've got to do first. Small, you go downstairs and call the telephone office. Ask Information for the number listed under the name of Elmira Kesselbrink, in Hagerstown, Maryland. No, don't call it—just find out the number. Randy, I want you to tell me some more about this man, Burns—everything you can think of."

The boy tried to recall all the conversations he had had with the suspected spy. He mentioned some of the silly questions Burns had asked—about track inspection, the number of soldiers in a troop car, and other unrelated matters. He listed the various states and countries the man had told of visiting, and his modest claim to a college education and the writing of verse.

"One thing about him surprised me," Randy concluded. "He had a lot more nerve than you'd expect in a bookkeeper. That day the rock came so near hitting us, I was plenty shaky. But it never seemed to bother him a bit. He just laughed and went back to work."

By the time the boy finished, Ben Small returned from the telephone booth in the lobby. There was a queer look on his round, sleepy face. "That number you wanted in

Hagerstown," he said. "It's 4-2881."

Harrow nodded. "That's what I expected." He smiled. "We're beginning to get the picture now. Let me give you the rest of the story. About the last of June we spotted a short-wave sending set in the garage of a cottage at Wildwood, New Jersey. That's a seashore resort down near the Delaware Capes. The cottage was owned by a retired baker named Eitel—a German, but he'd been thirty years in this country and had a pretty good record.

"We waited two weeks and couldn't pick up any messages coming from that set. But meanwhile we kept a watch on Eitel's mail. He got a couple of letters from Hagerstown. They were ordinary, newsy stuff about family affairs, sons in the Army, and so on. Then, last week, we found a lot of code numbers in invisible ink, written on the inside of the envelope flap. I recognized some of the numbers when I read this notebook, and I remembered that the letters were signed by somebody named Elmira Kesselbrink. So there you are."

"Hmm," said Small. "I got you. Burns was phoning his dope about troop movements and such to this Elmira—probably a woman. And she was relaying the figures to Eitel in her letters. Pretty smart."

"That's about the size of it," Harrow replied. "Now I'm

going back to Pittsburgh and go to work on this notebook. If we can get any decent prints, we may have a record of Burns in Washington. The name itself doesn't mean much. It's an alias—no doubt of that. So far you haven't any lead on where the fellow might be hiding. Keep the station covered and warn the yard men to be on the look-out for anyone of Burns' description trying to jump a freight. And one other thing. You might cultivate that telephone office some more, Small. Those calls to Hagerstown were probably made at night, from a pay-station. It's upwards of a hundred miles away and I doubt if many Hagerstown calls go through from here. Their records ought to give us a tip on where he went to do his phoning, and it's possible he'll try it again."

"That sounds reasonable," Ben Small agreed. "I'll get right on the job. I guess we don't need Randy any more, do we?"

"No." Harrow smiled. "Go ahead back to your section gang, young man. You've done a mighty good job. Keep your eyes open and let Small know if you see anything else that looks fishy."

He rose to shake Randy's hand and the boy left with a glow of pride and importance. That feeling was soon dissipated when he reached the cut. It was nearly ten o'clock and the heat was growing more and more intense. The sweating men and women working on the track looked at him resentfully, and Dan Leary's greeting was gruff—"Come on, b'y, get yer pick an' shovel an' make up fer lost time!"

Randy worked with the rest until the noon whistle sounded, then got his lunch-pail and went to sit by himself in the shade. He could catch bits of low-voiced conversation and sidelong looks from the rest of the group. Even Mike Hubka seemed to be avoiding him. He smiled grimly to himself. This was tough treatment, but he knew it was better for them to suspect him of having run afoul of the law than to guess his real errand. As long as the section boss understood, he was willing to take it.

The still, heavy air lay like a load on his shoulders when he started back to the track. There was a gray haze over the top of Big Calico and he hoped his father's prophecy about the weather would soon come true. Any change— even rain—would be better than this heat.

They were working far up the grade, where the big curve had been cut out of the mountainside. Behind them the wooded hill slope dropped away to Blacksnake River, a thousand feet below. And across the tracks the red shale cliffs rose almost vertically toward the crest of Big Calico. Perched on the fill beside the outside down-bound track there was a small board shelter, open in front. It housed a telephone box and a chest for emergency tools. Randy saw Dan Leary look often toward the little building in the next hour, and just as often at the hazy sky.

It was nearly two o'clock when the first rumble of thunder came ominously from the west. The pressure of the air changed suddenly. The heat was as oppressive as ever, but Randy felt an electric tingle along his skin as if all the little hairs were standing on end. The clink and scrape of shovels stopped all at once. Every member of the track gang was looking up in uneasy suspense.

"Hey, there!" roared big Dan. "Back to work, all av yez! There's no storm yet!"

They went at it once more, but in half-hearted fashion. When Randy stole a glance at the mountain he saw a gray-black wave of cloud rushing eastward, blotting out the sun. Where they stood below the cliff not a breath of air stirred, yet that mass of cloud was torn and tortured by a mighty wind. They could hear the howl of it through the Gap, and see the trees writhe under its force, high on the crest of the mountain.

Dan Leary laughed. "All right—ye've been wantin' to loaf the day long. Now bring yer tools an' get under cover. The little shack yonder will have to hold us all."

The gang needed no urging. They grabbed their shovels, picks and tamping-irons and ran stumbling along the ties. It was a tight fit when they reached the shelter. The women were given places at the back, where they could sit on the tool-box. The men crowded in under the overhanging roof. Then came the first whipping gust of wind. It picked up the dust from the road-bed and whirled it into their faces.

Choking and covering his eyes, Randy heard the rhythmic pounding of wheels on the rails. As it drew nearer he looked out and saw a big freight engine coming fast down the grade. It was No. 722 and there was no train behind it. His father must be deadheading down from the Gap to pick up a westbound freight. For a brief instant he saw the grim, goggled face in the cab window, and then the rain came in a lashing flood.

Before the boy could crouch deeper under the shelter the air was filled with blinding, livid light and a thunderclap almost shattered his eardrums. One of the women at the back of the hut began to sob and pray.

At that moment, with a slow, gathering roar that was

104

more terrible than thunder, a mass of rock broke loose from the cliff face and came crashing downward on the tracks. The slide was a good hundred yards below them, but it shook the earth under their feet.

Disregarding the downpour, Dan Leary sprang out from under the shelter. Randy was right at his heels as he ran down the ties. "A bad 'un!" bellowed the old man through the sheets of rain. "Two tracks blocked. Got to flag the westbound trains!"

They turned and fought their way back to the hut. "If this telephone line's still workin'," said big Dan, "I'll get a call through to the tower. Randy, get a flag an' torpedoes out o' that chest. Ye're the fastest one here an' ye'd better prove it now!"

The engineers who built the mountain division were brave and determined men. They drove the line through to Calico Gap seventy years ago, with crowbars and gunpowder and a reckless courage that refused to be licked. They blasted the grade out of mountainsides that fought them for every yard. And though at last they won a precious foothold for their rails, they never wholly vanquished that mountain enemy. Today the section gangs still wage guerilla warfare with the overhanging rock.

IX

The section hands scrambled out of the way and Randy opened the box. It was so dark that he had to fumble a moment before he found all he needed. With the furled red flag under his arm, and a spiked flare and two torpedoes in his hands, he plunged out into the deluge once more.

Pounding down the grade, he wondered whether wet torpedoes would explode under an engine's wheels. He was trying his best to protect them, but the water poured down his arms in streams. He passed the ugly brown mass of rock on the tracks and ran on, his feet slipping on the wet ties. When he opened his mouth for breath the water beat in and half strangled him. It was all like a nightmare.

Through the blur of rain he could see only a few yards down the track, and the only way he could judge how far he had run was by the weariness in his legs. He stopped and looked back, but the gray curtain shut off his view of the slide. He had one foot on a westbound rail and suddenly he felt a throbbing through the sole of his shoe. Somewhere down below a train was on its way up the grade.

Randy clipped one of his torpedoes to the wet rail and

galloped on another fifty yards before he set the second one in place. As he laid his hand on the rail he could feel the pulsing vibration of oncoming wheels. It even seemed to him that he could hear the engine's exhaust through the roar of the rain.

Hastily he tried to light the fusee by scraping its head along the iron. When nothing happened, he struck it sharply against the rail and saw it fizzle and steam. That was all. The red flare itself refused to light. He flung it aside and tore on down the track. The cloth of the flag was so wet that he had to work it loose from around the staff as he ran. Then the wailing hoot of an engine sounded, so close it brought his heart into his mouth. He leaped to the outer track and started waving the red flag.

The blunt, black nose of the locomotive loomed enormous out of the gray and at that instant there came a break in the downpour. For those few seconds the boy saw the puffing engine clearly—saw the engineer's face at the cab window—saw his look of sudden surprise, as he glimpsed the frantically waving flag—saw his hand shoot over to the airbrake lever. It was a passenger locomotive, tall and clean-lined like a thoroughbred, with giant 80-inch driving wheels. And grinding to an emergency stop behind it were the long

Pullmans of the road's crack "Westerner."

The conductor, resplendent in gleaming buttons and blue broadcloth, leaned from the door of the third car. "What's the trouble?" he shouted through the slackening rain.

"Big rock slide ahead," Randy called back. "It's across both up-bound tracks. Can you send a flagman back? My flare got wet an' wouldn't light."

"Okay, son," said the conductor. "We're seven minutes late, but you can't argue with a slide. Want to come aboard an' dry out?"

"Thanks," Randy answered, "but I've got to get back with the gang."

He saw the passenger brakeman start down the track as he returned toward the slide. The engine had stopped four or five hundred feet short of the debris that blocked the line and had run over the first torpedo without exploding it. He took the other off the rail and threw it in the ditch.

Dan Leary and his crew were working like beavers on the slide, but Randy could see at a glance that the mass of rock was no pick and shovel job. The rain had almost stopped now, but rivers of water from the drainage ditch dammed by the slide were tumbling across the four-track line. The gang's main effort was to prevent a wash-out at this point.

The foreman hailed Randy as he came up. "Good job, b'y," he panted. "The telephone line's out, an' we've got to let 'em know some other way. There's a freight comin' down now. Could ye ride her to the tower an' pass the word? We need a work train up here quick, so don't let 'em get on that Number One track."

Quickly the boy repeated the orders and splashed across to the eastbound side. The long coal train coming down the grade had slowed almost to a stop as it neared the scene of trouble.

"Safe to go through?" shouted the engineer, and Randy gave him the highball signal with his arms. "Got to get to the tower," he yelled back. "Can I ride the cab?"

"Sure—catch hold," the hogger answered.

Randy pulled himself aboard as the air was released and the locomotive began to pick up speed. The fireman motioned to his bench on the left side of the cab, and the boy took a seat on the edge of it, trying not to get the leather cushion wet.

"Looks like a bad 'un," the fireman commented. "Who flagged the varnish?"

"I did," Randy told him. "An' I really mean 'flagged.'

The way it was raining the fusee wouldn't light an' the torpedoes wouldn't pop. If it had been down-grade he'd never have got her stopped."

"Them slides can sure play hob," the ashcat nodded. "I was firin' on the Northern Pacific once, comin' down through the Cascades with ninety cars o' fir timber. A chunk o' the mountain peeled off an' landed smack in the middle o' the string. That train come apart so quick all we felt was a jerk, an' there we was, rollin' down the grade with forty cars. The hogger got religion, right then. Half a minute earlier an' that engine would ha' been part o' the mountain."

The engineer slowed again as he approached the yard tower and signaled with two short blasts of the whistle. Randy raced across the tracks and started up the ladder-like stairs. When he neared the top an assistant towerman opened the trapdoor and peered down at him. "Where you goin'?" he asked. "Nobody's allowed up here—only on railroad business."

"I reckon that's what this is," said Randy. "I've got a message for your boss from Dan Leary. There's a rock slide across both westbound tracks an' the telephone line isn't working."

The assistant's jaw dropped. "Come on up," he answered

hastily. "The chief's talkin' to the Dispatcher's office right now."

He motioned the boy forward and the towerman put a hand over the telephone mouthpiece. "Make it fast, son," he urged. "What's up?"

Randy told him in as few words as possible and the man nodded. "Okay," he said into the transmitter. "Get this. Number One and Two tracks blocked by a slide halfway up the curve. Yes—43's stalled, but okay. They flagged her just this side. Tracks Three and Four are clear. Leary needs a work train and the big scoop on Track One. Give me the word as soon as you start routing anything west on the outside tracks."

He pulled a couple of the levers in the complicated board in front of him and swung back to Randy. "Thanks, son," he said. "You look a bit wet. There's hot java back there on the stove. Help yourself to a cup."

Randy had been shivering a little, and the steaming coffee was a comfort. He drank it gratefully and went to the glass front of the tower for a look down the yard. He could see a big freight engine bumping over the switches to couple on to a three-car work train with a power shovel on the head end.

"Guess I'd better run," he told the towerman. "I'll ride back with the work crew. Thanks for the coffee!"

He hurried to the ground and sprinted across to the track where the work train was making up. The sun broke through flying clouds in the west and glinted brightly on the wet rails. As he neared the locomotive he heard his name called and looked up to see Buck Weeks grinning at him from the cab.

"Gosh!" Randy exclaimed. "I didn't see it was you. Suppose the driver'll let me ride up the line?"

"I don't dare ask him," laughed Buck. "Come on aboard. Ol' 722 ought to seem like home to you."

Randy saw a twinkle in his father's eye as he climbed to the gangway, but the big engineer pretended to be too busy to notice his passenger.

"How'd you get the word so quick, about the work train?" the boy asked.

"We saw the slide start," Weeks replied. "I looked back just as that rain caught us, an' saw the rock all over the right-o'-way, so we figured they'd need some machinery up there. That fall didn't miss us by much, did it?"

"About three seconds," said Randy. "An' I reckon if you'd still been there, some o' those flying rocks might have made it uncomfortable."

The switches opened ahead of them and the burly loco-motive hustled its three-car train up the grade at an emer-gency clip. The shovel's bulk hid the track ahead but a brakeman rode high on the top of it and waved them on with hand signals.

As they rumbled past the stalled "Westerner," Randy saw the frowning faces of passengers at the parlor-car win-dows. Stuffy-looking men held watches in their hands, and the boy could imagine their grumbling comments at the delay.

Buck Weeks laughed. "Bet they're havin' a fit," he said. "But they won't have to stay here long. The Dispatcher'll back 'em down to a cut-over an' send 'em up Number Three, soon as he's got a clear track over the hump. Most o' the folks on that train won't ever know that if they'd been on time they'd ha' been right under that pile o' rock!"

The brakeman's arms went out and down in a "slow" signal and a moment later they clanked to a stop. Randy jumped down and ran ahead. The section hands were doing their best to clear the second track, but they had made little headway so far. Dan Leary shouldered his pick and climbed over the rubble to confer with the boss of the work crew.

Already the big Diesel engine was lowering the shovel for an experimental bite into the slide.

"Hould it!" roared Leary. "Where d'ye think ye're goin' to throw that stuff?"

"Over here," said the other man, pointing to the ditch.

"Faith, an' didn't they have the sense to give ye cars to load it in? How'll the water drain off wid the ditch full o' rock?"

"Keep your shirt on, Dan." The work train conductor grinned. "With only one track to use we gotta do the best we can. Soon as the slide's cleared we'll bring up cars an' clean out your ditch. Go ahead, Tom—start shovelin'."

The big scoop made short work of the fifty-ton pile of rock and earth. Old Dan watched its progress and looked gloomily at the towering cliff above. "I niver trusted that place at all, at all," he told Randy. "This slide is only a little one—just a crumb off the cake, ye might say. Some day that big hunk o' mountain up there's goin' to break loose. I hope I won't see it, for that'll be a real slide. There won't be a wheel turnin' for a month while they dig out from under."

Four o'clock came and went and still the gang worked. The shovel carried away the heavy boulders, but could not get down to the track itself. The final clearing was done by hand, and it was nearly six o'clock when the rails of both westbound lines were fit for traffic.

Randy's arms ached as they tossed the last shovelful of earth on the pile that filled the ditch. He put his tools aboard the section trailer and said good-night to his tired mates. His father had long since taken the work train back to the yard, so the boy walked a mile or more down the curve to reach the path that led toward home. A dozen or more up-bound trains had been backed up in Gaptown during the afternoon and they were beginning to move now—preference freights and passenger trains storming up the grade, one behind another.

The boy watched them with a feeling of pride. He had done his part in starting those impatient monsters on their way west, and once more the high iron throbbed to their mighty tread. He turned up the steep path and climbed slowly, wishing the chores were done. As he came out at the bend of the road a farm truck rattled toward him and he recognized one of his neighbors at the wheel.

The farmer waved and stopped the ramshackle old vehicle. "Climb aboard, Randy," he said. "Give ye a lift as far as the house. Ye look sort o' tuckered out."

Randy got in, glad of the chance to sit down.

"You folks been bothered with tramps lately?" the man asked as he started up again. "Reason I asked, we had some come to our place this mornin'. Leastways I guess they was tramps. I was out in the field an' didn't see 'em, but these three fellers come up to the kitchen door an' asked for somethin' to eat. They offered to pay, but my ol' lady told 'em they was welcome to a couple o' quarts o' milk an' a loaf o' the bread she was bakin'. I wouldn't have encouraged 'em if I'd been on hand."

"Did she say what they looked like?" Randy asked.

"Yeah—she claimed one was tall an' thin an' another short an' stocky. The third feller done the talkin'. He was about my build, she said. Big, heavy-set man with a brown hat on. The others was bareheaded."

"I don't know whether they've been to our house yet," the boy replied uneasily. "I hope they didn't bother Mom. They don't sound like the kind o' people we want around."

He got out of the truck at the gate and thanked the farmer. But as he walked up to the house the description of the three strangers kept running through his head. The first two had a familiar sound. And the third? He wondered if Ben Small or Harrow, the F.B.I. man, would laugh at him if he told them what he was thinking.

*The coal that drives the trains and fires the steel fur-
naces and heats the homes of Pennsylvania has lain
under those mountains a long time. More than twenty
million years ago, the jungles of giant tree-ferns grew
there in vast swamps under a blazing sun—died and were
buried deep beneath new jungles through the ages. Then
the sea overflowed them, forced them down under the
terrible pressure of its depths, and piled a mud floor
hundreds of feet thick above them. Afterward the earth
heaved upward, throwing off the sea, the mud hardened into rock and the mountains were formed. But in
their hearts they still held the sun in those masses of
decayed vegetation, compressed through millions of
years into rich, black carbon.*

X

"Tell me, Mom," said Randy at breakfast next morning, "did anybody come to the house yesterday?"

"Only old Mrs. Simpkins, wanting to buy eggs," his mother replied. "What's on your mind, lad?"

"Nothing much. I heard there were some tramps asking for food up the road, an' I wondered if they'd stopped here."

Mrs. MacDougal snorted. "Small pickings they'll get at my door," she announced firmly. "With all the war jobs crying for men, I've no sympathy for them that would rather beg their bread."

"Atta girl, Mom!" Randy laughed. "You tell 'em where to head in. I may be a bit late tonight, for I've got an errand in town. I'll try to ride home with Jeannie, though."

The section gang had plenty to do that day, repairing the damage done by the storm. Most of the traffic was still being routed over the two outer tracks, while the shovel dug out the ditch and filled strings of dump-cars with muddy shale. By afternoon all traces of the slide had been removed.

Randy rode back to town on the rail-car at four o'clock, and hurried over to the Allegheny House. The clerk treated him with more respect this time. Mr. Small was in his room, he was told, and if he liked he could go right up.

The detective's squeaky voice answered his knock, and he went in. As usual, Small was lounging in the rocker, his fat sides overflowing its wide arms. He looked up from the afternoon paper and nodded sleepily.

"Come in, MacDougal, come in," he said. "Have a chair. Not quite so hot today, thank goodness. Any news for me? I think perhaps I've got a bit for you."

Randy sat down. "I don't know whether you'd class mine as news," he said. "But I figured it might be better to tell you. Remember the two men I was talking about—the tall, thin one an' the short, wide one who went down through our pasture an' left the footprints? Well, a pair like that called at a farmhouse on the mountain yesterday and asked for something to eat. But there was another fellow with 'em who did the talking. An' the way the farmer's wife described him, he was a pretty good-sized man, heavy-set, an' wore a brown hat.

"I know that's not much of a description, but it might fit Burns, if he's still in this part o' the country."

He waited for some expression of interest, but the detective merely nodded again in that half-awake way he had.

"The name," he said, after a moment, "isn't Burns, by the way. At least that's only one of his names. We checked back on a Pittsburgh address he'd given the Roadmaster's office and he was known as Byron while he was there. It's entirely possible he's taken to the woods with that couple you mentioned, though the description doesn't prove a great deal. It would fit about one man in ten around here."

The fat man paused and rocked impassively while Randy waited. "I found out one thing," he continued, at length. "It looks as if you were right about his going into that saloon of Bronsky's. The telephone office had a record of four calls made to the Hagerstown number from a phone at that address—all in the last couple of weeks. The police have got a man watching Bronsky's place now."

That seemed to be the end of the conversation, so Randy rose. "I'll let you know if I see or hear anything more," he said. "Maybe I'll have a chance to go up the mountain Sunday and I'll be on the watch for those three tramps."

"Good enough," said Small. "Keep out of sight if you can, though. I imagine your friend Burns wouldn't be very glad to have you recognize him. And that reminds me— better send a message if you want to talk to me. In case Burns has friends in the neighborhood I'd rather you weren't seen coming here."

Randy left feeling somewhat disappointed. From what Joe Roan had told him he had expected action and excitement when Ben Small got on the job. The man was exasperating in his calmness, and nothing important seemed to happen. He wondered a little about the detective's hint that he should avoid being seen at the Allegheny House, but he recognized the sense in it. Burns might suspect that he had picked up the red notebook and it was just as well if he didn't know Small or Harrow had been brought into the picture.

The rest of that week passed quietly enough. The weather held clear and hot. The big freights and troop trains moved on schedule. And the section gang found plenty to keep them busy under the keen eye of old Dan Leary.

On Sunday as soon as he got home from church, Randy changed into old clothes and helped his mother pack an extra-big snack, for he hoped to share it with Stan Lukowski. Before noon he and Babe were on their way up Big Calico.

There was a place on the mountainside, a mile to the northward, where fire had swept the forest a few years before. Randy knew there were blueberries in that burned tract and he thought they should be ripe by now. That was why he carried a six-quart pail as well as his parcel of lunch.

He knew of no trail leading directly to the burned-over area, so he angled upward through the woods, bearing always to the right. It was the roughest kind of going. There were dense thickets of evergreen, tangled briars, windfallen trees and rocky outcrops to slow his progress.

Once Babe, who had run a short distance ahead, gave a short, sharp bark. He hurried forward and heard her whimpering anxiously. When he burst through the brush the setter was standing on point at the foot of a sunny ledge. Following the direction of her outstretched nose he saw a thick, mottled coil among the rocks ten feet away. Then he heard the crisp whirr of the rattler's tail and saw its blunt, evil head lift and sway.

There was a broken limb by Randy's feet and he picked it up, tested its strength and went cautiously forward. The setter was quivering from nose to tail-tip but she held her point.

"Steady, girl," he murmured as he passed her. "Hold it. Don't move." He raised the club then and the snake started slithering away into the rock crevices. With a bound, Randy brought his heavy stick down across the dark, scaly back.

The rattler struggled and thrashed but it could not escape. Three times more he struck before the writhing snake lay still.

To make doubly sure, Randy smashed its head with a rock. Then he opened his jackknife and cut off the twelve rattles at the tip of the tail. As he proudly held up the trophy, Babe came leaping to his side, her red tail wagging with joy.

"Good girl!" He praised her. "You find 'em an' I'll kill 'em. Only watch out you don't get any closer'n that."

They emerged, ten minutes later, among the blackened stumps of fire-blasted trees. The rough slope was covered with berry bushes, some in thick patches on the ground, others standing breast-high, and all loaded with big blue fruit. Randy placed his lunch safely in the crotch of a birch sapling and went to work.

It was a berry-picker's paradise. Apparently nobody had been there before him, and the clusters had ripened evenly with few green berries left. He could roll them off the stems in handfuls, and in a matter of minutes the blue torrent had mounted in the pail till it was nearly half full.

"Pretty swell, eh, Babe?" he asked the dog. "When Mom sees these she'll want me to come again. An' think o' the

pies we'll have to eat!"

At that moment a loud, metallic clang made him jump. It had come from the pail in his hand. He looked about him, startled, and as he did so the tin rang again and the pail jerked at its wire handle. Then he heard a peal of mischievous laughter and a tousled thatch of sun-bleached hair bounced up from behind a bush a dozen yards away.

"Hi!" called Stan. "What's the matter, Randy?"

"Why, you—you—" Randy sputtered. "What you got there—an air rifle?"

"Better'n that," Stan laughed. He held up a Y-shaped sling-shot, and came nearer. "This here's my little 'un," he explained. "With the big 'un I'd ha' knocked that bucket clean out o' yer hand."

Randy set his pail down and examined the sling-shot with interest. "That's a honey," he said. "Hazel wood, isn't it?"

"That's right. I cut 'er down in the swamp, back o' the mine dump. An' the rubber—that's from a good inner tube —pre-war stuff. Want to see some shootin'?"

"Sure," said Randy. "S'pose you could hit that burnt tree down there?"

"The one with the woodpecker hole up near the top? Well—maybe. Here goes."

The boy took a pebble out of his pocket and fitted it to the rubber band. He seemed to sight, pull back and let fly all in one casual motion. The little stone flickered swiftly through the air and struck the target, thirty yards away, with a solid *tunk*. A fluffy gray bird with a red head popped hastily out of the hole and flew off toward the woods.

"Say!" Randy exclaimed with a chuckle. "You *are* good with that thing—scared Mr. Woodpecker right out of his nest. Come on an' help me fill this pail, an' we'll go over the mountain. I planned to pay you a visit today."

Stan was an expert berry-picker. His brown hands stripped the sprays at lightning speed and Randy had to hustle to keep pace. In ten minutes the pail was full to the brim.

"I got a bucketful myself this mornin'," the young Pole remarked. "Left 'em over there by that tree where you parked yer grub."

He led the way back to the birch clump and picked up a twelve-quart milk-pail heaped with blueberries. "I'd been here most o' the mornin'," he explained. "Just gettin' ready to leave when I saw you an' the dog, so I thought I'd watch you awhile."

Randy laughed. "You're a regular Indian," he said. "I

never dreamed there was a soul here, an' even Babe didn't spot you."

"If you'd come a little sooner, you'd ha' found two of us," Stan replied. "There was a pretty good-sized bear over the other side o' the burn, but he went off when he got wind o' me. Babe knew I was here, too, only she didn't bark. We're friends now."

They left the burned patch and climbed steadily through the woods till they reached the crest. There was a little breeze coming up from the other side, and Randy picked a cool spot under the trees where they had a view of the valley.

"I'm hungry," he told Stan. "What say we eat here? I brought some extra grub along. Sort o' figured I might run into you."

When they had finished the sandwiches and cake and given Babe the left-over scraps, they sat and talked awhile. Randy told the other boy about the pair of strangers he had seen crossing the pasture.

"They were the same ones you talked to, all right," he said. "An' it looks like they've picked up a third man now. He's older—a big, heavy-set chap. The three of 'em were at one of our neighbor's, trying to get something to eat. You haven't seen 'em again, have you?"

Stan shook his head. "No sign of 'em over this side," he answered. "But I'll be watchin'. I'll send you word by that freight-shack friend o' yours if they turn up. Come on, I'm thirsty. There's a spring down there a ways. Let's go."

The west slope of the mountain was new country to Randy. It was, if anything, rougher and wilder than his own side. About halfway down they found the spring—a tiny stream of cold, clear water bubbling out of the rocks. They drank their fill and continued the descent, while Stan pointed out places of interest in the valley below.

"That spur track over there runs to the Calico Mine," he explained. "You can see the pit head, where the track turns in past those trees. That's where my dad works. An' down below is Doran. The Polish church is the one with the cross on top o' the steeple. It's St. Stanislaus—my name saint. We all went to early Mass there this mornin'."

Half an hour later they were down on the valley road, a narrow, twisting strip of concrete that formed the main street of the coal town. Dreary-looking little frame houses huddled close on either side. Most of them were two stories high and either backed up against the foot of the hill or perched above the steep slope that ran down to the river.

The tiny dooryards were bare, trampled earth.

Randy thought he had never seen a place so bleak and ugly, but Stan seemed to be proud of his village. A few miners sat smoking their pipes on the front steps and he nodded and spoke to each one by name. Swarms of scantily clad children peered out shyly at the stranger from windows and house-corners.

Stan's home was at the upper end of the street. The house was gray and weathered like the rest, but there were three geranium plants in the front windows.

Stan led the way in. "Mom," he called, "we got company," and Randy saw a tall, blonde woman standing in the door that opened into the kitchen. She smiled, showing a mouthful of strong white teeth.

"This here's Randy," said the Polish boy. "He comes from over the Gaptown side an' he works on the railroad. We been up on the mountain together."

Mrs. Lukowski welcomed the visitor in broken English, and exclaimed over the big pail of blueberries Stan handed her. Three or four small brothers and sisters appeared from nowhere and stared at Randy with wondering eyes. They were neatly dressed. As he looked around, the boy realized that the house was as spotless as his own.

Stan took him out to the backyard and showed him some of his treasures. There was a young raccoon in a wire-fenced enclosure, and two gray squirrels in a wooden cage.

"I had a bear cub last year," Stan told his guest, "but he got too strong. Busted out one night an' killed the Liskas' pig. We never did catch him."

They went down the bank to the rocky creek-bed and sat there talking awhile in the shade of the willows.

"I've got to start back pretty quick," Randy said. "It's been nice seeing your place, Stan. Before I go I think I ought to tell you that those two fellows you saw on the mountain are probably bad eggs. With this third one I told you about they may be planning some sort of sabotage on the railroad."

Stan's eyes grew wide. "Golly!" he breathed. "You mean like blowin' up bridges or wreckin' trains?"

"That's about it," said Randy. "I've got reason to believe they're enemy agents—getting their pay from Hitler. An' I'm afraid they're smart enough to keep clear o' those soldiers that patrol the Gap. So if you see 'em, or come across anything that doesn't look right, send me word as quick as you can. I know how to get in touch with the F.B.I."

"Boy—that's the G-men, isn't it? You bet I'll send you word. An' I'll watch that mountain every day. Wouldn't it be sump'n if we could help catch 'em!"

Randy grinned and held out his hand. "I'll be counting on you," he said. "Now I'll see if I can find your trail up to the ridge. So long, Stan."

He picked up his pail of berries, called Babe to his side, and started for home.

They call them "P" trains—the Preference Freights that
go thundering down the rails, carrying essential products to the waiting ships. They hold right of way over
all other traffic, and they run on schedules that would
make an old-time railroad man gasp. Mighty passenger
engines pull them—engines that can pick up a fifty-car
block of tanks in Detroit at sundown and put them on
a Hoboken dock by noon of the next day. The crews
of those trains have done a war job just as surely as the
men building the bombers and the guns.

XI

Randy could probably have found his way alone over the mountain, but with the red setter to guide him it was easy. Babe followed the same course they had taken coming down. She stopped at the spring and lapped a drink from the little stream that flowed from it. Hot from his climb, Randy sat down in the moss and ferns and lifted the water in his cupped hands. While he rested there a moment the dog bounded off up the hill. She was out of sight when Randy rose to follow, but he could hear the rustle of leaves where she ran along the hillside above him.

Suddenly she barked twice. Knowing her voice as well as he did, Randy knew she wasn't excited. It was merely her way of announcing something—the same bark she used when the mail-carrier's car stopped at the rural delivery box at home. He hurried up the slope through the brush and whistled to let the dog know he was coming.

"What's the trouble, girl?" he called.

"Reckon I'm the trouble, kid," a drawling southern voice answered. And a few yards up the hill Randy saw the glint of sunlight on a bayonet. The soldier slouched with his back against a tree, but the rifle in his hands looked like business.

"Hi," said Randy. "You patrolling the mountain?"

"That's right. Orders to keep civilians out o' here."

"I'm just on my way home," the boy replied. "I live down the other side, on the Gaptown road."

The soldier shook his head. "Too bad," he said, "but you cain't go acrost tonight. Might as well trot back down thar an' find some other way 'round."

Randy was exasperated. "Look," he pleaded, holding up his pail of berries, "do you think I'm an enemy or something? Nobody stopped me coming over, an' it's fifteen miles around through the Gap."

"Yank," drawled the man in uniform, "I'm right sorry for you, but I'm supposed to shoot anybody that don't obey that order. I kin shoot pretty good, too."

The boy stared at the lean, brown, humorless face and saw that argument would get him nowhere. "Okay," he said, "I'll go 'round. Come on, Babe."

But the setter was no longer in sight. She had gone on over the ridge and was headed for home. He whistled and called several times without any response, then turned on his heel and started down the hill.

All the pleasure was gone out of his day. If he could

catch a freight starting up to the Gap from the west, he would be lucky to reach home before dark. And while he could not help appreciating the Army's zeal in guarding the mountain-top, it seemed to him they might have applied a little common sense in his own case. Babe worried him, too. Suppose some nervous recruit heard her in the brush and took a shot at her. He stopped and listened and whistled again, hoping she might have come back to find him. But the woods drowsed in the late afternoon silence and no distant bark answered him.

He reached the valley road at last and trudged southward. Several cars passed headed toward Doran but there were none bound in the direction he was going. It was three miles down the road to the place where the main line crossed. He could see the high viaduct against the sunset long before he reached it. The valley narrowed at that point, and the four-track way crossed it in a flying leap on great piers of steel and concrete.

When he got to the foot of the viaduct he had to climb once more by a steep path that led up the side of Big Calico to the rails. A short distance up the grade there was a broad siding where the helper engines waited, and Randy was cheered by the sight of two big black freight hogs sitting there with steam up. That meant a train was due soon. He sat down on the embankment with his pail between his feet.

A hundred-car string of empty oil tanks clanked down the grade, westbound, and a third engine uncoupled to back into the siding behind the first two. Then he heard the long-drawn hoot of a freight locomotive from the mountainside across the valley. It was a "P" train, rocketing out of the curve into the straightaway approach to the viaduct. She hit the high bridge at forty miles an hour and hardly began to slacken speed till the locomotive passed the place where he sat. Then he could hear the hiss of air and the cars rolled by more and more slowly.

He could see then why the train was a preference freight. Three flatcars near the head end carried giant electric generators. Behind them came olive drab Army tractors, big as elephants. Then forty-foot steel landing craft with high, square bows that would let down to form ramps. There were sealed boxcars, too, with the warning placard, "Explosives: do not hump." That was an order switchmen understood and respected.

The long freight was just coming to a stop when the red caboose finally went by. Randy got up and went toward the rear platform, where the hind-end brakeman was beckoning the kicker engine up from the siding. The boy showed his section hand's badge.

"You reckon I could ride over?" he asked. "I live down the other side, just beyond the curve."

"Get aboard," the brakeman answered. "You'll find the Big O inside, an' he'll tell you if it's all right."

Randy went in through the passage and past the narrow steps leading up to the cupola. On the stove at his left, as he entered the main compartment, he saw the ever-present pot of coffee steaming. The conductor, sometimes called the "Big O" or "Big Ox" because of the capital "O" on his Order of Railway Conductors' card, was seated at his folding work-table, writing up a train report. He wore no gold braid, just overalls and jumper and a battered felt hat. But there was authority in every line of his seamed and weathered face.

"Yes?" he said, glancing up.

Randy repeated his request. "My father's a freight engineer," he added. "Big Ross MacDougal. He runs a helper engine out of Gaptown."

The conductor nodded. "I know him," he said. "Sure, you can ride. I wouldn't try jumping till we get to the yard, though. Not if you want enough o' those berries left to make a pie!"

Randy grinned. "I'd like to give you some," he said. "I'll see if I can find a dish an' put 'em in your ice-box."

"That'll be fine." The conductor nodded. "I like blueberries with sugar an' cream, an' I'll get a chance to eat some on the way to Harrisburg."

There was a jarring bump as the helper engine hooked on behind. Then came the sigh of released brakes, the short, panting roar of the exhaust and the click of couplings as the train began to move again.

The shack came in from the platform and gave Randy a bowl from one of the lockers. When it was filled with berries and placed in the refrigerator the boy followed the brakeman up into the cupola. There was a thrill in being up there, where he could command a view of the whole train, that almost equaled riding in the engine cab.

In the fading light he could see the rough, black "V" of the Gap, and the laboring locomotive, three-quarters of a mile ahead.

"Funny thing," said the brakeman. "I don't suppose you notice it, livin' right here all the time, but Calico Gap is a place I've never liked. Takin' a train over, I mean. Right about here I always tighten up, like I was afraid o' somethin'. An' when we're past the curve an' headin' down for Gaptown I breathe a lot easier."

Randy looked at him. He was a steady-eyed, square-jawed fellow of thirty-five or more—certainly no imaginative youngster.

"You mean the rock-slides, maybe?" the boy hazarded.

"Maybe. But there's somethin' else. I get a feelin' that perhaps men bit off more'n they could chew when they tackled these mountains—as if the big curve had no business to be there, hangin' onto the side o' the cliff. Still"—he laughed—"it's been there quite a spell now, and an awful lot o' trains have been up an' down that grade. I reckon I'm just notional."

They were in the jaws of the Gap now, and Randy felt some of the other man's uneasiness as he stared up at the dark woods, reaching skyward on either side. The head end of the train eased over the crest and swung out of sight to the left, going into the big curve. Then another long freight came puffing around the bend from the east. For the minutes it took to pass them there was too much noise for conversation. And when Randy spoke again they were already rolling down the curve.

"I'd better get below," he said, "an' be ready to bail out

if there's a chance. I want to get home before dark."

"Okay, kid." The brakeman grinned. "I'll be thinkin' of you tonight when I eat those berries. So long now."

The train began to slow down for the yard soon after it left the curve, and Randy found being on the hind end an advantage. The caboose was rolling hardly more than fifteen miles an hour as it passed the hill path. He held the pail of blueberries at arm's length and swung off, spilling only a few as he lit running on the ties.

He walked across the tracks, found the trail in the half darkness and started climbing. His legs were weary, for he had done plenty of tramping that day—most of it, it seemed to him, uphill. When at last he reached the top the last light was dimming in the sky and the trees made dark pockets of shadow along the wayside. He walked up the middle of the narrow road, wondering if his family had been worried by his lateness. Babe must have reached home at least an hour before, and the fact that he wasn't with her might have caused some concern.

That thought made him start to run. He was almost at the edge of the farm clearing when two men stepped out of the bushes right in front of him. It was so dark he almost bumped into them.

"Hey, where you goin'?" one of them asked in a low voice.

Randy stepped back a stride, startled at the question. "I'm —I'm going home," he stammered.

"Yeah? Where's that?"

"Right up there," the boy pointed.

The other man spoke then for the first time. "Good! He's der vun, Choe—hold him!" And before Randy could dodge they had him, one by each arm.

"What is this?" he asked, choking with anger. "If you guys are after money, I haven't got but a quarter on me."

"Just stand still an' keep yer mouth shut," growled the first man. He was short, squat and very strong, and while he gripped Randy's arm with one hand he began a thorough search of his pockets with the other.

"Here's the quarter," he announced, and tossed the coin scornfully into the road. "Knife, handkerchief—what the devil's this?" There was a dry rustling sound from the snake rattles, and the fellow jerked his hand out hastily.

"Naw," he muttered in disgust. "That's all there is. He ain't got it on him, Fritz."

The other man snarled something under his breath—something that sounded like an oath in a foreign tongue. He was a head taller than his companion, and more slimly built. His hair looked pale in the starlight. "Vait yet!" he snapped, and began feeling of Randy's shirt around the waist. Then he stooped, explored the rolled-up bottoms of his dungarees and shoved a finger into the tops of his hiking boots.

"Bah!" he exclaimed at last. "Let him go. Ve get it an-odder vay."

The short man thrust his face close to Randy's. "Get goin'," he commanded. "Don't run. Walk. An' don't do any yellin'. I got a gun here an' I don't mind usin' it. Now start."

The boy stumbled forward under the push of his hand. He walked steadily toward the house. The pail, half-filled with blueberries, still hung foolishly from his fist. He could see the light in the kitchen window now, and the thing that had just happened seemed wholly unreal. Yet the muscles of his left arm still ached from the stranger's grip. He stopped and looked back, but the road was empty.

Suddenly he knew what it was the pair had been looking for. The red notebook! They were the same men he had tracked in the pasture—the same ones who had been in Lew Burns' company, asking for food. Burns wanted his note-book but didn't want Randy to see him. So he had sent his two pals to stage the hold-up.

His head was in a whirl as he opened the kitchen door. To his relief, his mother was sitting calmly by the table darning socks.

"What kept ye, lad?" she asked.

"I went over the mountain," Randy told her. "Paid a visit to a kid I know over in Doran, an' it took me longer to get home than I'd figured. Did Babe come in?"

"Aye, she's been here since sundown. Your father was away or I'd have sent him to look for ye."

"I got you some blueberries," the boy remarked, trying to sound casual. He set the pail on the table. "Well, guess I'll do the chores. Got anything to eat, Mom?"

"I milked the cow myself," Mrs. MacDougal answered. "There's a cold roast and bread and butter and milk aplenty. Ye look tired, son. Better be off to bed early."

"All right," said he. "But if you're sitting up to wait for Dad I wish you'd bolt the door. I saw a couple o' tramps, down the road."

The Indian names still cling to places in the Pennsylvania mountains like echoes of long-silent voices. Warrior's Mark and Conemaugh, Juniata and Osceola and Kittanning, Punxsutawney and Daguscahonda, Neshannock and Venango. Except for a rare flint arrowhead turned up by the plowshare, those names are all that is left of the shadowy, copper-skinned savages who used the whole vast region of the Alleghenies as a hunting and fishing ground. But sometimes a boy, wandering those woods and valleys, finds that his feet are following a very old trail, forgotten perhaps for centuries. And he knows he is walking in the moccasin-prints of warriors.

XII

Randy was up early Monday morning. As soon as he finished the chores he went upstairs and knocked at his sister's door. "Are you dressed, Jeannie?" he asked in a low voice.

"Yes," she answered. "Come on in, Ran."

"I wanted to talk to you alone for a minute," he explained. "I've got to get word to a man that I want to see him tonight. Could you call him up for me when you get to the office? His name's Ben Small and he's at the Allegheny House."

Jean looked surprised. "Why, I've heard of him," she said. "Isn't he a railroad detective? Joe Roan knows him."

"That's right," replied Randy. "But don't let that worry you. It's nothing to do with me. I've got some information he ought to have. You just tell him I'll be walking along the street near the hotel tonight at four-thirty."

"Well," the girl said doubtfully, "I'll call up for you. But it seems to me, whatever this is, you ought to tell Dad about it."

"I will, sooner or later. Only right now he'd probably think it was all nonsense. Don't forget to phone, now." And whistling his favorite "Casey Jones," he went down to breakfast.

That afternoon the boy could hardly wait to finish work and start for his rendezvous with Small. He found he was ten minutes ahead of time when he reached Main Street, and walked along slowly, idling in front of store windows and staring at the merchandise like any country boy in from the hills. Out of the corner of his eye, however, he kept a watch on the people who passed.

He was standing on the street corner a block from the hotel when he saw the mammoth shape of the detective sauntering slowly in his direction. Small came up beside him and teetered on the curb waiting for the traffic light to turn green. The man did not look at him but spoke softly from the side of his mouth.

"Go down two blocks to the Little Daisy lunch wagon," he said. "Order something. I'll be there."

Then the light changed and he moved majestically off, crossing the street like a ship under full sail. Randy turned and strolled south as directed. A gaudy sign pointed the way to the "Little Daisy Diner—Giant Hamburgers Our Specialty," and he was soon inside. Business seemed to be dull at that hour. There were no customers on any of the stools, and the girl behind the counter was yawning and polishing her bright red fingernails.

Randy perched himself on a stool and ordered coffee and doughnuts. While he was stirring the cup the door opened and Ben Small stepped in. He tested the creaking stool next to the boy's before settling his weight ponderously upon it.

"Oh, hello," he remarked in his squeaky voice. "Didn't see it was you." Then he gave his order to the girl for a stack of wheat cakes.

"That'll keep her busy at the other end of the counter for a while," he murmured. "What's on your mind?"

Randy recounted his adventure of the night before, keeping his voice too low for the cook to hear. "I'm pretty sure it wasn't money they were after," he finished. "The way they talked it was some particular thing, an' small enough to be hid in my pockets. I think it was Lew Burns' notebook."

"You pretty certain they were the same two men you told me about?" asked Small.

"Yes," Randy answered. "I haven't had a chance to look for tracks, but they sure looked like the same pair."

"All right," said the detective quietly. "It's a good sign. If Burns thinks you picked up the book and still have it, that means he doesn't suspect yet about your reporting to me and Harrow. Only trouble is, they may try breaking into your house to get it."

Randy nodded, sober-faced. "That's what worries me," he said. "They've got a gun."

"Well," the detective told him, "I doubt if they'll try any rough stuff yet. And I'm expecting a call from Harrow tonight. I'll tell him, and see if he wants us to take any steps."

He slipped a quarter into Randy's hand as the girl approached with the stack of wheats. The boy placed it on the counter and got his change. Then he dunked the last piece of doughnut, finished his coffee and rose.

"So long, son," Small nodded. "Tell your Uncle Abner I was asking for him."

Randy chuckled as he went up the street. Small's elaborate precautions made him think of an old-fashioned gangster movie. But when he remembered the pages of figures in the little red book, and the black shape of the gun in the short man's hand last night, it didn't seem so funny.

Jean came out to the barn that evening while he was milking. "I just wondered," she said, "whether you met your Mr. Small. They had to send up to his room to get him when I telephoned, and he sounded sleepy. I didn't know whether he understood me or not."

"Everything was okay," said Randy. "I talked to him, an' I guess we can forget the whole business. It wasn't anything very important anyhow."

"Well, then I should think you could tell me," she wheedled.

Randy laughed. "Blamed if that isn't just like a girl," he said. "Always full o' curiosity. I'll give you the whole story some time, Jeannie, but not just yet. You'd better go back in or you'll get that barn smell you're always telling me about."

He heard Babe bark once in the night, but when he went to the window there was nothing moving in the dark yard. The dog made no more noise, and after a few minutes Randy went back to bed and to sleep.

To reassure himself, before he went to work the next morning he looked around the house and yard. Daylight revealed no sign that anything had been disturbed. He decided a rabbit must have hopped past the setter's kennel and roused her in the night.

Down at the section house he found Dan Leary whetting scythes and sickles.

"Ye're goin' to turn farmer today, b'y," grinned the big Irishman. "The grass up there looks like a hay-field, an' if we was to get a dry spell we'd have some bad fires."

"That's all right with me," Randy responded. "I've swung a scythe since I was ten years old, so I reckon I can keep up with your gandy dancers."

The rest of the crew were less enthusiastic about the job. They were used to handling crowbars and spike-mauls, but cutting grass brought different muscles into play. Old Dan kept them at it with his jibes and jokes, and by noon they had mowed nearly half a mile of bank on both sides of the right-of-way.

When they quit for lunch one of the old-timers stretched his back and grimaced painfully. "I ain't felt so done in since Spanish War days," he groaned. "Guess I never did tell you fellers 'bout the greatest hog-'rastlin' in hist'ry, did I? Well, that was one time I was really tuckered."

He eased himself down on the mowed grass and opened his lunch box. His story was told between bites of a huge ham and cheese sandwich.

"Ham," he mumbled. "There was years when I couldn't stand the taste of it, after that day I was tellin' about.

"You see I was a kid fireman on a little two-engine branch line in Florida. Wouldn't take me in the Rough Riders, so I lied about my age an' got the job firin'. Reckon I was the puniest little bakehead that ever chucked pine knots in a wood-burner.

"Well, we was haulin' meat for the troops in camp. Meat on the hoof. This partic'lar day we had six carloads o' hogs—them Florida piney-woods razorbacks—meaner'n wildcats. This line of ours run along the edge o' the Everglades. A lot of it was on pilin', with water all around. We was poundin' along at ten miles an hour, an' just as we come off the trestle onto a little round island the door on one o' the stock cars let go. I looked back an' seen hogs jumpin' out all over the place. The engineer slammed the brakes on but by the time we got stopped the whole train was past the island an' out over the water again.

"The shack come runnin' up over the cars with orders from the Big Ox. There was nothin' for it but to back up an' get them ornery shoats aboard. Well, sir, that island was no bigger'n a baseball field, an' the hogs was racin' 'round an' 'round it like crazy. We had to roll back by inches to keep from hittin' 'em.

"Then the real job started. All of us—even the fat ol' engineer—piled out an' started chasin' them danged animals. There was no lumber to make a gangway up to the car. Every hog had to be caught an' lugged over there an' the door shut after him. A couple of 'em started to swim for it, but the alligators had gathered 'round when they heard the squealin', an' they didn't get far. Did I say squealin'? Man, that ain't no name for it! Folks heard that racket clean over on the beach, twenty miles west.

"It was the middle o' the forenoon when we started, an' the sun was settin' by the time the last hog was in the car. Makes me ache all over jus' to think of it."

Old Dan chuckled. "It must ha' been a foine day's wurrk," he agreed. "I kin see now why labor has been distasteful to ye iver since!"

. . .

Randy was still swinging his scythe that afternoon when a freight rolled eastward down the mountain. Suddenly a rock as big as his fist dropped in the grass at his feet. It had a piece of paper tied around it with a string. He looked up in time to see Joe Roan waving back to him from the top of a box-car.

Stooping, he picked up the stone and removed the paper. A message was scrawled on it in pencil, smudged and difficult to read. At the top was the word—"Tuesday." Below was written:

"Randy I hope you get this becus their is somethin gone

on up on the mounten. I will show you tonite if you come up I will be waiten at the place ware you seen me that first time remember? I will be their at seven oclock. Be sure to come Stan."

Randy's heart beat faster as he thrust the paper in his pocket and set to work again. Stan's message meant action. He would have to hustle to reach the appointed place by seven, even if he went without supper. Ordinarily it took an hour and a half to climb Big Calico. Meanwhile, it seemed to him he ought to tell Ben Small where he was going, but there would be no time to hunt him up in town.

Just before four o'clock the boy drew Dan Leary aside. "Would you do a favor for me, Dan?" he asked. "I want to get word to that railroad detective, Ben Small, tonight, but I've got to start for home right away. Could you take a note to him?"

The big section boss looked at him sharply and then smiled. "Ye're in no trouble, are ye, Randy?" he said. "All right, then. I'll see the fat man gets yer note. Where is it?"

Randy wrote hastily on the bottom of the crumpled sheet that had come from Stan. "Dear Mr. Small," he scribbled. "I'm going up on Big Calico tonight to meet the boy who wrote this. I don't know what he has found, but I think maybe you will be interested. I'll be home by ten if you can come to my house. R. MacDougal."

He folded the note and gave it to Leary. "You'll find him at the Allegheny House," he said. "I'm sure obliged to you. Maybe Small will explain if you ask him."

Big Dan shut one eye and nodded. "That'll be up to him," he said. "I'll ask no questions."

Randy reached the farmhouse at four-thirty and changed into his hiking clothes. "I'm going to get the milking done early," he told his mother. "I want to go out a little while tonight."

But early milking was more difficult than he had expected. The cow was eating grass at the far side of the pasture and resented being driven in before her usual time. It was only with Babe's help that the boy was able to get her up to the barn. It was nearly six o'clock before he brought in the foaming pail.

In the kitchen he ate a few mouthfuls of bread and butter and downed a glass of milk. Then he went out. Babe was eager to accompany him and he hesitated a moment before tying her up. "Sorry, girl," he told the dog, "but I'm afraid

155

you'd bark an' make trouble. You stay here an' take care o' the place."

It was cloudy that evening and twilight came early. As Randy hurried up the mountainside the woods were already dark and shadowy. Twice he missed the blazes that marked his trail and had to waste time hunting for them. A flashlight would have been a help, but he had none and he had decided against bringing a lantern.

"Shucks," he told himself, "the Indians used to cruise all over these mountains, night-time the same as in daylight. An' I ought to know Big Calico as well as any Indian."

He had no watch with him but he knew it must be after seven o'clock when he approached the last steep pitch. Stan, he had no doubt, was waiting impatiently somewhere on the other side of the ridge. In the last few minutes it had grown so dark that he was no longer sure he was on the trail. All he could do was climb straight up the hill and trust to luck. When he got to the summit he thought he was enough of a woodsman to locate the spot where he and the Polish boy had first met.

Five minutes later he stumbled up a stony ledge and found no hill in front of him. He must be on the crest. But where?

He could see no familiar landmarks in the darkness under the trees. A cold, damp wind blew over the mountain and it felt as if rain might be on the way. Randy shivered as he felt his way forward, step by step. For the first time he began to have doubts about the wisdom of this expedition.

Wars are no longer fought merely by armies, navies and air forces. The curse of human hate and suffering and bloodshed involves whole populations, reaches into homes and factories, tears at the foundations of all civilized life. The effort on each side is to destroy the production and transportation that enable the enemy to keep on fighting. And so the vicious circle must continue until the day when all peoples join to make a final end of wars.

XIII

Randy was sure that it must be long after the appointed time. He wondered if Stan had given up waiting and gone home. Perhaps if he whistled loudly enough the Polish boy would hear him. But that might get them both into trouble. So far he had been lucky in keeping clear of the armed guards who patrolled the ridge, and he knew there was real danger of being shot at if they heard his signal.

He tried again to find some pattern in the grouping of the trees that would show him where he was. For a moment he thought he remembered a big, lightning-shattered spruce that was dimly outlined against the sky. There had been such a tree a little to the north of the place where he sat that Sunday afternoon when he first saw Stan Lukowski. Keeping the spruce on his right he crept forward once more.

Just ahead of him there was a brush-covered knoll, and instead of climbing over it, he swung to the left, expecting the going to be easier. He had taken half a dozen cautious steps around the base of the little hill when a glimmer of light came up to him from the hollow beyond. It was no more than a faint, yellowish glow reflected on the leaves.

Sometimes it almost disappeared, then flickered up again.

Randy crouched low and moved down the hillside toward the light. He felt his way along, placing his feet so carefully that not a twig snapped. If someone had built a fire he knew it was likely to be one of the soldiers, and he had no intention of being caught.

The last few yards he crawled on his belly, inching forward a foot at a time. And finally the entire hollow below was in view. Raising himself on his elbows he could see a tiny fire burning in the lee of a ledge of rock. In front of it were the dark shapes of two men, kneeling, feeding the flame with sticks. They seemed to be cooking something over the fire in a small pan.

Neither of the men was in uniform, but beyond that he could not be sure. For a moment, when he caught the glint of firelight on tow-colored hair, he thought one of them might be Stan. Then he recognized something familiar in the broad, squat build of the other man. He was looking at the backs of the same skulking pair who had waylaid him on the road forty-eight hours before!

The fact registered in Randy's brain with a jolt. He drew a quick breath and a tingle of excitement went through him.

This was his chance to find out what they were doing on the mountain. Unobserved, he could watch every movement they made. He was just wishing Stan could be there to share his thrill when a stick broke with a soft crunch close behind him. He rose to his knees and looked around.

"Stan?" he whispered. "Is that you?"

No voice answered from the darkness, but something moved there—a bulky shadow, blacker than the surrounding black. Randy caught the sound of heavy breathing and started to his feet in terror. Before he could make a move the shadow lunged toward him.

The boy acted by instinct. In a split second he twisted his body to the right and dove headlong, and his assailant passed so close he felt the brush of a hand on his shoulder. Squirming through the brush, Randy regained his feet in an instant. He no longer thought of silence, only of escape. But at the first step his toe caught in a tangle of vines and he was thrown to the ground once more.

His unseen foe was on him with catlike quickness. He felt heavy hands grappling for his throat and heard a panting snarl as he fought to get clear. Then suddenly he saw a million shooting stars and passed into roaring, empty blackness.

Winter, thought Randy. Sort of early this year, but cold—bitter cold. He didn't really want to wake up because he would be still colder then. Perhaps he had been sick. There was a dull, aching throb in his head, a ringing in his ears. The bed felt hard and uncomfortable. Maybe if he pulled up the covers he could get warm. But his groping hand found no blankets—only bare, rough earth and his own naked body.

With an effort he opened his eyes. It was dark around him, but not the dark of night. Full consciousness was returning to him now and he began to remember. Stan's message . . . the climb up the mountain . . . two men by the fire . . . a struggle with someone he could not see. Strangely enough he had not been killed. He was alive and naked and the place he was in seemed to be a dirt-floored cabin. There were no windows—only an old door that hung askew on broken leather hinges and let in the gray light of morning.

Painfully he lifted himself and staggered to his feet. He felt faint and dizzy, but above all he was shaking with the cold. The clothes he had worn were nowhere to be seen. Thinking they might have been dropped somewhere outside, he pushed the door open and stumbled across the threshold.

The woods around the hut dripped dismally in a light, steady drizzle of rain.

Shivering, Randy made a half-hearted search of the brush near by, then hurried back to the shelter offered by the cabin. There was a crude fireplace at the end opposite the doorway, but he could find no wood to burn in it. Even the matches he carried in the pocket of his jeans were gone, along with his clothing.

In desperation he started thrashing his arms around him and dancing to restore the circulation in his legs. There was a lump on the side of his head that felt like a hen's egg, but the painful throbbing was less noticeable now.

Gradually his brain began to function. Why, he asked himself, had he been left here with nothing to wear? The answer must be that the man who had knocked him out wanted to be sure he didn't leave for a while. And who was that man? If he had been the companion of the pair in the hollow, standing guard while they boiled coffee, Randy was pretty positive he was Lew Burns.

So he was dealing with three men—spies, saboteurs, or both—almost certainly enemies of his country. And the fact that they had taken away his clothes, rather than leaving someone to watch over their prisoner, meant that all three of them were busy somewhere else. The idea frightened him, but it also made him angry. He determined then and there that he would fool them, even if he had to run the mountain naked in the rain.

Or was he on the mountain? He had never seen this ramshackle hut before, and there was no way to tell how far they might have carried him after that blow on the head. He looked out the door again, but the trees grew close on all sides and overhung the rickety roof. Then he remembered something Stan had told him. This must be the cabin the Polish boy said was "ha'nted."

The walls, he saw, were of logs and very old. The moss and clay with which they had once been chinked had long since fallen out. Mice and squirrels had gnawed the ridgepole and the hand-split shakes that formed the roof were curled and twisted by years of weather. It had been built a long time ago—perhaps by some buckskin-clad hunter of frontier days.

Through the open door Randy could see a thick clump of oak saplings, and the clusters of big, green leaves started him thinking. In a moment he had pulled the top of one of the young trees down and stripped off dozens of leaves, each one larger than his hand and tough as wrapping paper.

Once, when he was a little boy, he had helped Jeannie make "rugs" for her play-house by stringing oak leaves together. The knack of it came back to him now. He began punching the stem of one leaf through the center of another and twisting it under the mid-vein till it pierced the leaf again on the other side. In ten minutes he had put together a coarse fabric of overlapping leaves, two feet wide and more than a yard long.

They were still wet and clammy to the touch, but when he draped them around his middle he was no longer undressed. A string of ground creeper, threaded through the top row of leaves, made a serviceable belt to hold the improvised kilt in place.

The boy was still far from warm, but his spirits had risen with the sense of doing something. His dizziness was gone now and he began to realize he was hungry and thirsty. There was a little pool of rain water in a depression under the eaves. He knelt there and drank enough to wet his parched tongue and throat. Just as he was rising his eye fell on something half buried among the fallen leaves. It looked like a pinkish clay cylinder an inch and a half in diameter. He picked it up and looked at it more closely. It was a broken stick of dynamite!

Startled, Randy put the stick down and backed off a few steps. He knew enough about explosives to realize that wet dynamite, away from fire, was harmless. But finding it there was a shock. His memory flashed back to the Sunday when he had met Stan Lukowski—the bit of copper wire he had picked up in the ashes where two of these same men had camped. If their mysterious business had to do with dynamite and wire, it was time for him to act, and there wasn't a moment to lose.

First of all he had to find out where he was. On the ridge just above the cabin there were tall spruces that might afford a view of the country around. He scrambled up the slope, scratching his bare legs and torso in the brush. Fortunately the biggest tree in sight had branches only seven or eight feet from the ground and he was spared the ordeal of trying to shinny in a leaf skirt. He swung himself up and mounted swiftly till he was a good fifty feet above the ridge.

Clouds and fog lay about him over the treetops but he could still make a fair guess as to his location. Northeast and southwest the long hump of Big Calico loomed below him in the mist. And when the clouds broke for a moment he could see the sharp outline of the cliff, two miles to the southward, where the mountain dropped off into the Gap.

For a moment he clung there in the high crotch of the spruce, searching the shaggy terrain in all directions. To spot anything as small as a man, down there in the forest, would have been next to impossible. But he still had a slim hope of locating help. Yesterday he had done his best to steer clear of soldiers. Now no sight would have been more welcome than a moving dot of Army khaki.

The mist closed in again and the evergreen boughs showered his bare back with chilly raindrops. He shook himself and scrambled down the tree. From the moment he had seen that stick of dynamite there had been a fear somewhere at the back of his mind. Explosives, in the hands of Burns and his gang, could have only one purpose. That would be the destruction of the single big military objective in the area—the four-track rail artery through the Gap.

For a fleeting second Randy pictured the thing they might be doing even now—the great curve with trains rolling east and west—his father's engine doubleheading a long freight up the grade—the sudden blast at the cliff-top, and thousands of tons of loosened rock crashing down.

It was too terrible to think of. Trembling, the boy started to run, and his bare feet took him southward toward the Gap. For the first few hundred yards he made good time.

Then the rough going slowed him up. A sharp stick tore the sole of his right foot and made every step an agony. Bitterly he thought of the toughened pads that made Stan's progress through the woods so easy. But wishing would get him nowhere. He gritted his teeth and limped on.

Perhaps he grew a bit lightheaded. Hunger, the damp chill of the rain, his injured foot and the persistent ache from the blow on his skull combined to give his thoughts a feverish quality. Once he imagined Ben Small was with him and he heard his own voice urging the fat man to hurry faster. Then again it was the hard-faced mountaineer soldier from the South who loped along at his side, drawling, "I kin shoot pretty good, too." But there was no panting detective—no businesslike Garand rifle to back him up. He was all alone.

When he heard Stan's voice he thought it was another of those fever dreams and struggled on without answering. But it came again: "Randy—hey, Randy—where the heck you goin'?"

He stopped where he was and brushed a tired arm across his eyes to clear away the mist. And out of the woods slipped a real flesh-and-blood boy who stared at him with open mouth and wide, scared eyes.

When Alfred Nobel invented an explosive called dynamite, in 1886, he multiplied the destructive force of gunpowder thirteen times. He knew that in the right hands his discovery would be one of the greatest gifts ever made to mankind; and in the wrong hands, a tool that could increase war's frightfulness and spread horror through the world. He was a good man. He hoped for the best, and lived to see his invention used to forward the greatest era of construction in all history. But the evil possibility of its misuse troubled him to the day of his death. The Nobel Prizes he bequeathed for outstanding contributions to literature, medicine, physics, chemistry and world peace are monuments to one man's conscience.

XIV

"Wh-what happened to you?" Stan gasped. "Where are your clothes?"

Randy tried to grin but he could not keep his teeth from chattering.

"Reckon I lost the trail last night," he said. "Anyhow I missed you. An' then I ran into those Nazis. While I was watching two of 'em, another one came along behind me an' conked me on the head 'fore I could get away. When I came to, my clothes were gone an' I was lying in that old shack back there. Then I found a busted stick o' dynamite they'd left, an' I figured I had to do something quick, to stop 'em. That's where I'm heading now—over to the cut above the big curve."

"Gosh!" said Stan. "You look terrible, an' you must be about froze. Here"—he stripped off the old slicker he was wearing—"put this on. It'll keep the rain off you, anyhow."

Randy wrapped the garment around himself gratefully. "You haven't got anything to eat, have you?" he asked.

The young Pole shook his head. "Wish I had, but I left in too much of a hurry. Didn't you get any supper last night?"

"Only a couple o' bites," said Randy. "I was late an' had to hustle if I was going to meet you."

"Gee—an' I thought all the time you hadn't got my note! I waited a long time. Then I scouted around tryin' to find those three guys again. I'd seen 'em in the mornin'—that was why I sent for you. But they'd cleared out. After a while I went down an' it was past ten o'clock when I got home. What makes you think they've gone over to the cut? Did you find a trail?"

"No," Randy admitted. "I didn't even think to look. I just had a hunch an' started."

"Well, I'll see if there's any tracks. This ground's soft, an' they must ha' left some. You wait here. Say—what's wrong with your foot?"

"Nothing much. I stepped on a sharp stick is all. I'll keep up with you—after I've rested a minute."

He sat down on a fallen log and held his aching head in his hands. Meeting Stan had cleared his brain and given him fresh courage. But he was still weak. When he looked up again the other boy had vanished and the woods were lonely as before. He listened, but wherever Stan had gone he was making no noise. There was only the soft rustle of dripping leaves and once, far away, the muffled hoot of a freight engine on the grade.

Suddenly a twig crackled faintly and he heard a sound of movement in the brush, down the hill to his left. Randy ducked behind the log and crouched there on all fours. Somebody was coming—somebody a lot less silent-footed than the woods-trained Polish boy. He waited, tense and motionless, while the sounds grew nearer. Then there came an eager little whimper and a patter of running feet, and over the log bounded Babe.

The setter was panting and there were burrs tangled in her red coat. She sniffed at the unfamiliar slicker, then huddled against him, her tongue licking frantically at his neck and ear.

"Good girl!" he whispered. "You came to find me, soon as they let you loose, eh?"

He got up and sat on the log again, fondling the setter's silky ears and pulling burrs from her hide. After three or four minutes Stan reappeared, noiselessly as ever.

"Company?" he chuckled. "She's got a good nose if she found you way up here. We don't need her to track those spies, though. They left a trail anybody could follow. An' you're right—they're headed toward the cut!"

"Let's get going then," said Randy. "Only first I've got an idea. Maybe we could send Babe home with a message, if there was any way to write it."

Stan chewed on his knuckles and thought for a few seconds. "I got it!" he exclaimed. Pulling a big jackknife from his pocket he began hacking at the weathered end of the log where the bark was gone. In a moment he had split off a broad brown chip. With a few quick strokes of his knife he cut letters in the wood—"H-E-L-P." Then, beneath them, he carved another letter—"R."

"Here," he said, holding out his arm. "Tear the sleeve out o' my shirt. It's an old one anyway."

Randy ripped the sleeve off at the shoulder seam and Stan tore the cloth into two long strips. "You use one o' these to tie up your foot," he suggested. "Here—lemme see that cut."

He examined the wound and wiped the blood away with his own strip of cloth. "It'll be sore," he announced, "but 'tain't deep enough to worry about. I figger a little red won't hurt on this message we're sendin'—maybe make 'em think it's important."

He wrapped the chip up in the blood-smeared rag and tied it firmly to the setter's collar. "Now," he said, "can you make her mind you?"

Randy took the dog's head between his hands and spoke to her earnestly. "You've got to go home, Babe," he said. "*Home.* Understand? Go on, now—straight home."

Her sad brown eyes looked at him reproachfully and the wagging plume of her tail drooped. But she turned and trotted away down the hill without a backward glance.

"That's some dog," said Stan with respect. "Smarter'n a lot o' folks. Here, hold up your foot. I'll have a bandage on there in no time."

With the cloth bound tightly over the cut, Randy found he could walk almost as well as ever. He followed Stan a hundred paces or more to the westward and stopped where the other boy pointed to a track in the wet leaf-mold. It was a deep, sharp imprint, made by a heavy boot.

"There's two others with him," said Stan, his voice dropping to a whisper. "You'll see some more tracks a little ways along. This feller here was carryin' somethin' heavy in his right hand or on his right shoulder. See how much deeper he trod with his right foot?"

Randy nodded. "The trail looks mighty fresh," he said. "How long ago do you reckon they went by here?"

"Can't tell for sure. Maybe two or three hours. I'd say

right around daylight."

Stan led the way through the woods, his body crouched and his sharp eyes following the trail. The men had chosen the easiest way, skirting the denser thickets and avoiding the steep ledges. Once or twice they had stopped to rest.

It was at one of these places, where the grass was crushed as if a weight had been set down, that Randy had his first chance to compare the three tracks. Among the jumbled foot-prints he could pick out one made by a stubby, broad-toed boot and another that was longer and narrower. Without being able to identify them positively, he was pretty certain they belonged to the two men who had held him up and searched him—the two who called each other "Fritz" and "Joe."

The third track had been made by a fairly big man wearing sneakers. The ribbed rubber soles left an unmistakable mark on the wet earth.

"That's the guy that jumped me last night," Randy murmured. "The way I remember it he moved mighty quick an' quiet, as if he had on rubber shoes. Come on—we've got to keep going or we'll be too late."

The rain had stopped falling now, but the morning was still cloudy and cold. Stan plowed ahead and Randy limped doggedly in his wake. Once the Polish lad lost the trail on a bare outcrop of stone that ran along the crest of the ridge, but he picked it up again beyond, after a five-minute search. The boys moved quietly and kept to the cover of the brush as much as they were able. Both of them knew that any moment might bring them within sight of the men they were tracking.

"How much farther is it to the cut?" Randy whispered.

"Not far—less'n half a mile, I guess. Why? You gettin' tired?"

Randy shook his head. "I'll make it, okay. Only I don't want to run into 'em an' give ourselves away."

They crept along the side of a gulley and through a clump of spruces beyond. The cliff-edge must be close now, for they could hear the labored puffing of a pair of engines hauling a long train up the grade below. Suddenly Stan dropped on his stomach and reached back a warning hand. Randy crawled forward till he lay beside him.

"Look," Stan whispered. "Just to the right o' that big oak tree. See him? He's bendin' over somethin' on the ground there."

Peering through the leaves Randy saw a man straighten up and look cautiously about. He was fifty yards away, but there was no mistaking his tall, slim build and blond hair. The boy remembered him well. He was the one his thick-set companion had addressed as "Fritz."

Apparently the man was satisfied that no one was watching him, for he stooped once more and his arms moved as if he were tinkering with something the boys could not see.

"What's he doin'?" whispered Stan. "I can get a lot closer without him hearin' me. I want to get a look at that gadget he's workin' on."

Yard by yard the boy crawled forward and Randy wormed his way after him. There were some thick juniper bushes a little to the left, and Stan used them as cover for their advance. Soon they had reached a place where they could lie behind a screen of leafy brush and observe the man from a distance of only twenty paces.

"It's a car battery!" breathed Randy excitedly.

"Yeah," Stan answered. "An' that thing wired up to it—that box—you know what that is? It's what they set off a blast with!"

"Gosh!" Randy whispered. "I was right, then—about the dynamite!"

Stan nodded. "Look," he said. "You stay here an' keep an eye on him. I'm goin' to sneak around through the woods an' see if I can find the wires. Maybe I can cut 'em before they shoot the blast."

Before Randy could reply, the Polish boy had slipped silently off into the brush. He had been gone perhaps a minute when a noise of clumsy footsteps came from the woods to the south. That was the direction in which the cliff lay, above the railroad cut. Randy held his breath and waited. When the second man came into view, he was not surprised to see the squat, broad-shouldered, black-haired member of the gang.

"Hold it, Fritz," said the new arrival in a low voice. "He ain't ready yet. There's a troop train just startin' down. Say in about three or four minutes he'll give yuh the signal. All set, are yuh?"

"Ya," the other man muttered. "Noding can go wrong now."

"Okay," said the dark one. "We'll meet yuh at the car. I'm goin' back up where Lew is. I gotta see this!"

With that he turned and started back into the woods at a run. The fair-haired man fingered the plunger on the black box, then stood erect, rubbing his palms together nervously.

Randy measured the distance between himself and the saboteur. There was too little cover to allow him to crawl closer. He wondered if he could make the twenty yards fast enough to catch the man off guard. "Three or four minutes," the dark-haired thug had said—and the signal might come at any second. It was now or never. Shivering, he gathered his legs under him, ready to jump.

At that very instant Stan came back. There was a rustle of leaves at Randy's side and the boy from beyond the mountain wriggled through the brush like a snake. "I couldn't find the wire," he whispered breathlessly. "That guy come along an' I had to hide. What'll we do?"

"Wait!" said Randy. "I know! Your sling-shot— Have you got it?"

A light broke over Stan's face. "Sure!" he breathed, and reached swiftly for his hip pocket. "It's the big 'un, too. Look!"

The stout hazel fork he held up was a formidable weapon, fitted with a strip of thick, heavy rubber. From another pocket he produced a rounded stone nearly as big as an egg.

The tall saboteur was standing with his back to them, waiting for the signal to push down the plunger and fire the blast.

Without a sound Stan rose on one knee and took aim. There was a long second while Randy's heart seemed to stop beating. Then, with a *whoosh* the taut rubber was released. The stone flew through the air so fast Randy's eye could not follow it, but he heard the dull thud as it struck. The man called Fritz did not even raise his hands. His legs buckled under him and he slumped to the ground like a sack of coal.

"Come on!" cried Randy. He dashed across the intervening space and flung himself on the prostrate body of the spy. But Fritz did not struggle. The rock had hit him squarely in the back of the head and he was out cold.

Stan had his knife in his hand. With a couple of quick motions he slashed the lead-wires that ran from the firing box. And just at that moment the sound of a pistol-shot came from the cliff-top, off to the westward.

"*Production and transport of war munitions will never get started in America,*" *Goebbels told the German people.* "*Our network of sabotage is too strong.*" *The keenest and most ruthless brains in Naziland had organized that Fifth Column. Men trained for years in secret destruction—men who had lived in the United States and spoke the language without a trace of accent—men supplied with money, maps, codes and arms—all were ready when war began. But, to the eternal credit of the F.B.I. and its counter-espionage system, the German effort at sabotage failed. The nation proceeded to fulfill the greatest program of production and transportation in world history.*

XV

"That shot!" Randy exclaimed. "It must have been the signal from Burns! If there's no blast they'll be back here in a hurry to see what's wrong. We've got to fix things so they can't set off that dynamite. You hide the battery an' I'll tie this bird up so he won't make trouble if he comes to."

He took a twenty-foot length of the cut wire and bound the unconscious spy's hands firmly behind his back, then threw a loop around his ankles and hauled them up till he lay securely hog-tied. Stan meanwhile had unscrewed the battery caps, dumped out the acid and dropped the heavy box in a crevice between two rocks.

"Good," Randy panted. "That ought to stop 'em for a while. Now help me pull this Nazi back in the bushes."

They picked up the man's sagging body between them and carried it thirty or forty yards into the woods. There they found a thick clump of laurel bushes with glossy leaves that grew close to the ground.

"They'll never see him in here," grunted Stan. "An' he's heavy for a skinny guy. Let's park him an' crawl out where we can watch."

"All right," Randy agreed. "But remember—keep your head down. That fellow Joe packs a gun, an' probably Burns does, too."

They left Fritz in the laurel thicket and crept back toward their first hiding-place. Randy saw that Stan was lagging behind. "What's the matter?" he whispered.

"Tryin' to find another rock for my sling-shot," the young Pole answered. "Darn it—they're all flat an' rough-edged up here. Takes a round 'un to shoot straight."

They were both on their hands and knees, searching for a smooth stone of the right size, when the thud of running feet came from the woods ahead. They flattened themselves to the ground and looked out through the screen of brush.

It was the man Randy knew as Joe who came charging out of the undergrowth. His black brows were drawn together in an ugly scowl and he was puffing from his run. At the sight of the empty spot where his accomplice should have been he came to a staggering halt. His mouth dropped open in astonishment.

"Fritz—hey, Fritz!" he called in a low voice. Then he looked hastily about, as if he wanted to be sure this was the place. They saw his eyes fall on the ends of the clipped wires and he seized one in his hand, staring at it in unbelief.

183

As the meaning of what he saw dawned on the spy, he gasped out a choking curse. Obviously he thought the man, Fritz, had double-crossed his fellow plotters. With frenzied haste he began to rush back and forth, hunting for the battery.

"Look—he's found it!" whispered Randy. The man had stumbled across the crevice in the ledge and was grunting savagely as he tugged at something down there between the rocks.

"Won't do him no good," Stan answered. "All the juice is gone. But gosh! If I only had a stone I could nail him now!"

There was a quick stir in the leaves behind them and both boys turned their heads in panic. Through the brush raced Babe, her tongue out and her red sides heaving. She threw herself on Randy in an ecstasy of affection.

"Sh-h-h! Hush now, girl," he whispered, pulling her down beside him with hands that shook. But the saboteur was too much occupied with the ruined battery to hear the commotion of her arrival.

"That rag's gone off her collar," Stan breathed. "Darn it, I tied it on good, too. You think maybe she's been home?"

But Randy never got around to answering that question.

Even as he opened his mouth to reply, they heard a crashing in the brush and two men ran past them. The black-haired spy heard the noise, too. He whirled to face it, reaching for his hip pocket, but he was a second late.

"Put your hands up, Mister," one of the newcomers addressed him coldly. "Don't go for your gun. We'll take care of that."

Randy stared at the man who spoke. He had on a slouch hat and a belted raincoat, but the boy recognized the athletic build and the voice. It was K. P. Harrow, the F.B.I. man! He and his companion both held automatic pistols leveled at the saboteur's breast.

While they were disarming him there was more trampling in the brush and other men came into view. Two of them were soldiers with rifles in their hands. The third was Big Ross MacDougal. At the sight of his father's huge figure, Randy jumped to his feet and ran toward him.

"Dad!" he cried. "I thought you'd be out on your engine! Was it Babe told you where we were?"

The giant engineer turned and looked at him in open-mouthed amazement, then began to shake with laughter. "'Tis a braw sight ye are, laddie!" he chuckled. "What on airth ha' ye been doin' to yersel'?"

Randy looked down at himself and grinned. The tattered slicker hung open, exposing his bare stomach and legs and the oak-leaf kilt, now considerably the worse for wear. His father came striding over to him and seemed relieved to find he was not seriously hurt.

"Aye," said Big Ross. "Babe brought the message, but we'd already started when we met her. From the blood on the bit o' cloth it looked bad, so we've been hurryin'. The dog led us straight to ye."

"Just in time, too," Randy replied. "But there's something I've got to tell Mr. Harrow."

He hurried over to the Federal agent, who had finished handcuffing his captive. "They were going to blow up the cliff over the big curve," Randy told him. "There's three of 'em. We got another one an' he's tied up back there in the bushes. But Lew Burns is still loose—"

"Easy, there," Harrow interrupted. "Take your time and let's have the whole story, Randy. Who's this?" He pointed to Stan.

Randy told what had happened and introduced his companion. "He's better with a sling-shot than most folks with a gun," he bragged. "Hit Fritz square in the head with a rock just when he was going to shoot the blast."

"The kid's nuts," the black-haired prisoner snarled. "Fritz 'n' me was just campin' out up here."

"Suppose we take a look at this Fritz fellow," Harrow suggested.

Stan led the way to the laurel thicket and pulled the branches apart. The blond man lay on his side as they had left him, but he was groaning and his eyes were open.

"Hm," said Harrow. "You've got him trussed up pretty tight. Edwards, slack off on that wire and put the cuffs on him. Know who he is?"

"No," said the other F.B.I. man. "Do you recognize him, Chief?"

Harrow nodded. "We were watching him for a month in Pittsburgh. Then he gave us the slip. Come on. We've got no time to waste if we're going to catch Burns."

The two soldiers appeared to be under his orders, for he detailed one of them to take care of the prisoners. Then he hurried to the place where the cut wires lay among the leaves.

"Follow these up and see where they lead to," he told Edwards and the other soldier. "I'm going to scout around over here to the westward. You say that's where the pistol-shot came from, Randy?"

"Yes," the boy answered. "An' I heard Joe tell Fritz they'd meet him at the car. I reckon they've got one hid, somewhere down the mountain."

"I know where the nearest road would be," Stan volunteered eagerly. "Lemme show you."

He darted off into the woods and Harrow hurried after him while Randy watched with envy. "If it wasn't for this blame foot," he grumbled, "I could go with 'em."

Then he remembered his hunger. "Dad," he said, "you don't happen to have an apple in your pocket, do you?"

His father clapped a huge hand to the side of his jumper. "Weel, now!" he exclaimed. "I'd clean forgot. Your mither made me bring ye a bite to eat." And he hauled forth a bulky paper bag.

Randy grasped a sandwich in both hands and began wolfing it down as they followed the others along the trail of the wires. "I sure was starved," he said between mouthfuls. "What about Ben Small? Did he show up at the house?"

"Aye." Big Ross laughed. "He got your message, right enough, but not till midnight. Then he called the man Harrow and they drove up to the house early this mornin'. Ben started out wi' us, but the mountain was a wee bit too much for him. We left him sittin' on a rock halfway up."

Ahead of them they heard a low whistle. Edwards, the G-man, had found something. Through the trees they could see him standing on the top of the cliff, a short distance below the hill crest. Randy raced down the slope, careless of his injured foot.

"Look at that!" exclaimed the Federal agent. He had a loop of the wire in his hand and was scraping away loose earth and leaves from the ground. What he had exposed was a long row of holes, drilled in the soft shale, a dozen feet back from the edge of the rock. In each was a stick of dynamite with a detonator cap attached.

Gingerly the F.B.I. man began lifting them out and laying them in a pile. Big Ross gave him a hand with the job.

"There's fifty pounds o' the stuff here," the engineer growled. "Enough to blast out the biggest slide we ever had on the Gap grade."

Edwards nodded. "They must have drilled the holes for it months ago," he said. "We've had an armed guard on the mountain since April, and they'd have heard the noise of drilling. Let's see what Private Wilson's found."

Twenty paces to the west they came on the soldier, staring at a second row of blast holes. His face was grim. "I don't know what them pink sticks are," he said, "but I ain't touchin' 'em. They look like dynamite to me."

Edwards chuckled. "That's right," he replied. "But they won't hurt you unless there's current to set 'em off. We'll put the stuff back here where it can't do any damage, and your lieutenant can send a detail to carry it away. On our way back we'll reel up this wire. It's new. Maybe we can find out where they got it."

They returned to the place where the soldier stood guard over the two captured saboteurs and sat down to wait. When half an hour had passed Edwards began to grow fidgety. "The Chief may be in trouble," he said. "If they got to the car ahead of Burns they should have had him before this. I'd better go down there."

But before he had taken a dozen steps, Harrow and Stan appeared among the trees. They were alone.

"Missed him," Harrow told his assistant disgustedly. "We were close enough to hear the car start, but I couldn't get a shot at it."

He glanced at the prisoners and went on in a lowered voice. "We might get something that'll lead us to him when we question these chaps. Looks as if it was Burns, all right. What did you find over at the cliff?"

Edwards told him, and the Federal man's eyebrows went

up. "A hundred pounds of it, eh?" he said. "They really meant business, didn't they? Well, there's nothing more to do here. We'll take 'em down to police headquarters. I have to go back to Pittsburgh tonight."

With the big red setter racing on ahead, they started the descent of the mountain. A short distance down the side of the ridge they met a young lieutenant and three privates headed toward the Gap.

Harrow gave the officer a sketchy outline of the morning's events. "Thanks for lending us your men," he said. "We can take care of the prisoners from here. You'll want to post a guard over the dynamite, though, and it wouldn't be a bad idea to patrol that cliff above the curve. One of the gang got away and he might come around here again."

Stan left them there to go back to his own side of the mountain. "Reckon you'd better keep the slicker." He grinned at Randy. "You might scare folks without it. I'll be over an' pick it up some day soon."

Harrow shook hands with the Polish boy before he departed. "You and Randy have done a pretty fair day's work, I should say." He smiled. "I'm going to see that the Department hears about it. Any time you want a job as a G-man, when you've finished school, let me know."

Stan flushed with pleasure. "Golly," he said. "You mean that, Mr. Harrow? I—I'll sure do some studyin' from now on!" And he sped away over the hill.

The F.B.I. man turned to the prisoners. "By the way," he said sternly, "just what did you do with this boy's clothes?"

The man called Joe shrugged his shoulders. "I tell yuh I never seen the punk before," he growled. "Me an' Fritz was just campin' out—"

"Yes," Harrow cut in. "I remember. What was in the pockets, Randy?"

"My knife an' a handkerchief—maybe a piece o' string. I'd left my money home."

Harrow's deft hands went through the dark-haired man's pockets swiftly. "Is this the one?" he asked, holding up Randy's jackknife.

The boy took it and nodded. "It's mine, all right," he said.

"I guess that's all you'll get back," Harrow told him. "I've no doubt they burned the clothes or buried 'em. All right, let's get on our way."

They had gone about two miles when they saw a rotund figure struggling upward through the brush. It was Ben

Small, puffing like a porpoise, his moon face red and perspiring.

"I—I did my best," he piped in his high voice. "Haven't climbed a mountain in twenty years, an' I won't mind if I never do it again."

"Weel," Big Ross MacDougal laughed, "ye can turn around now. Ye'll find it easier goin' down!"

It was past noon when the party reached the farmhouse. Babe had dashed ahead to announce their coming, and Randy saw his mother on the back steps, shading her eyes with her hand as she counted them. She recognized him in spite of his limp and his weird costume. He saw her shoulders straighten with relief as she hurried back into the house to finish preparing a meal.

Harrow started to herd his prisoners into the car that stood in the dooryard, but Big Ross intervened. "Ye'll have to eat somewhere," he boomed hospitably, "an' it may as well be here. The wife'll ne'er forgi'e me if I let ye leave hungry."

The F.B.I. man sniffed the aroma of ham and eggs, biscuits and coffee coming from the kitchen door. "Mr. MacDougal," he grinned, "your invitation is accepted!"

Of all the machines contrived by man, there is none so grandly impressive, so vitally alive, as the steam locomotive. A ship has stately beauty and vast power. A transport plane has graceful, soaring speed. But in the brute bulk of a railroad engine—the flashing drive of pistons, turning mighty wheels—the deep, hoarse bellow of the exhaust—there is something akin to the human soul. Every boy and every man breathes quicker at the sight and sound of a big locomotive storming down the rails. The sleek, shining streamliner may be faster and more efficient, but it can never take the place of the old, black "iron horse" in the hearts of Americans.

XVI

Randy missed two days' work that week. For his own part he would have gone to the track the next morning but his mother was firm. As soon as Harrow and Small had driven off with their prisoners she washed her son's foot, doused it with arnica and put him to bed with a clean bandage. The lump on his head had gone down and the painful throbbing had departed. With a full stomach and the knowledge that the dynamiting plot had failed, he began to feel better.

But by the end of the second day he was restless. He had reread most of his favorite "Huckleberry Finn" and twiddled the radio dials for hours in an effort to get something besides soap operas. He picked up his father's "Book of Rules" and thumbed it through for the hundredth time. If he ever got the chance, he knew he could pass a railroad examination.

From where he sat in the parlor easy-chair, with his foot propped up on a stool, he could catch the ceaseless rumble of the trains. It was less like a sound than like a throbbing in his bones. And the wailing whistles of the great freights, muted by distance, were calls he found hard to resist. He wanted to get back to his job—to be where he could see and feel the rush of wheels over the high iron.

When the next day dawned he was up and dressed and had pulled on his shoe over the bandaged cut. He was careful not to limp as he passed through the kitchen on his way to the barn. And his mother, who understood railroad men, let him go without a word. He did the chores, ate breakfast and set off for Gaptown with his father and sister in the car.

Big Ross glanced at him out of the corner of his eye and let fall a casual remark.

"I was talkin' to the Master Mechanic yesterday," he said. "The road is short o' firemen an' they're thinkin' o' puttin' on a few learners. From what I gathered they won't inquire too carefu' into their ages. Ye know I was a month short o' seventeen when I started firin' mysel'."

Randy was too excited for speech. He sat there, gripping his knees, and let the words sink in. At last he trusted himself to ask a question.

"Wh-when can I make my application?" he stammered.

His father chuckled. "Ye needna worry!" said he. "I already put your name in. Time enough when ye've finished the week's work on the track."

Randy was walking on air as he crossed the yard to the

section house. Most of the gang had already assembled, and the rail-car was on the spur and loaded. Old Dan Leary's bushy eyebrows lifted as he noticed the boy's arrival.

" 'Tis a full crew we'll have, the day," he said, "an' a good thing, too, for there's plenty o' wurrk. Where ye been, b'y?"

Randy flushed under the eyes of the gang. "I got a cut in my foot," he answered. "Couldn't walk on it for a couple o' days. It's okay now, though."

He worked through the morning and as he was starting to eat his lunch beside the track the burly section boss strolled over to him. They were out of earshot of the others.

"It's none o' my affair," old Dan began, "but I was worryin' about ye, son. I did me best to give yer note to the road dick, but he wasn't there, so I left it wid the clerk. Whin ye didn't show up, I figgered there might be trouble. If ye need help, say so. I take care o' me b'ys."

Randy was touched by the big Irishman's anxiety. "You've been swell to me," he gulped. "There was some trouble, all right, but it turned out fine. All I can tell you is that we stopped a couple o' skunks who were trying to wreck the railroad. If we hadn't, you'd have been up against the meanest job o' track clearing you ever saw."

A look of relief spread over Leary's weather-beaten face. "Good b'y!" he exclaimed. "It's what I've been fearin' iver since the war started."

"There's one more thing," Randy said, and hesitated. "I think you ought to know this. That fellow Burns that used to work with us is a bad egg. He was in this an' he got away. If he ever shows up around here, I reckon you'll know what to do with him."

Leary's huge hand closed into an iron fist. "That I will," he replied fervently. "Ben Small told me that much, an' I've had me eye peeled for the dirty rat!"

Although he limped a little that day and the next, Randy's foot healed rapidly. On Saturday he drew his pay and went directly to the Master Mechanic's office at the end of the yard. With a pounding heart he stood in front of the wooden railing and gave the girl clerk his name.

She was new on the division and had a bit of trouble with the word "MacDougal." It was while Randy was spelling it out for her that the Master Mechanic himself swung around from his desk and came over to the rail. He was a big, stoop-shouldered, grizzled man who had been a first-class hogger back in the old days. His voice had the volume and tone of a locomotive whistle.

"MacDougal?" he roared. "Another o' those Mac-
Dougals? Well, we made engineers out o' Big Ross's first
two boys—maybe there's a bit o' the old stuff left over in
this 'un. Give him those two letters. I already had 'em made
out. One for the doc an' one for the rules examiner. Monday
mornin' we'll see if his innards are tickin' all right, an' how
much he knows about the book. Come back here after
you've passed 'em, son."

"Thanks, Mr. Halliday," Randy managed to answer, as
he took the two envelopes and shook the big man's extended
hand. Outside, he drew a deep breath. "After you've passed
'em," the Master Mechanic had said. Not "*if* you pass 'em."
He was counting on a son of Big Ross MacDougal to make
good, and Randy vowed then and there that he would never
let Halliday down. He could hardly wait to get home and
start brushing up on that rule book, for he was no longer
over-confident—only determined.

Sunday was a fine day, but he spent the afternoon under
the arbor, murmuring the answers to possible questions
under his breath. Babe barked and nuzzled his hand in vain.
If she expected him to go for a hike she was disappointed.

About four o'clock Stan came down the mountain. He
was more neatly dressed than Randy had ever seen him. His

straw-colored hair was combed and slicked down and he actually had on shoes!

"My maw told me I had to wear 'em if I was goin' to visit folks," the boy grimaced. "I hate 'em, but I reckon I'll have to get used to 'em if I'm goin' to be a G-man."

Randy told him about his own prospects of a job in the cab, then showed him the farm buildings and introduced him to his mother. Stan stayed to supper. When he departed, carrying the borrowed slicker, Randy went at his "Book of Rules" again.

About the time dusk fell his father came out and found him hard at it. "Listen, lad," he said. "Dinna work yersel' blind. The examination'll be easier than ye think. It's when ye go up for engineer that they get tough. What they want in a student tallowpot is a strong back."

Randy laid the book aside and stretched his arms. "I thought I knew it all backwards." He grinned ruefully. "Now I'm up against the real thing I'm not so sure."

However, he stopped worrying about it after that and got a good night's sleep. In the morning he put on his best clothes and rode down the hill with the others. Since the examining physician wouldn't be in his office till after nine, the boy went over to the section house first.

Dan Leary was there early, as usual. He took one look at Randy's Sunday suit and scowled. "Ye're quittin' the railroad?" he asked coldly.

"No, sir!" said Randy. "Not me. An' I may be back here begging you for a job tomorrow. But today I'm taking my exams for fireman."

The old Irishman's frown changed to a delighted grin, and he caught the boy's hand in a bone-crushing grip. "Begorra," he said, "an' it's proud o' ye I am! O' course," he added loyally, "there's no part o' railroadin' to match the track work, but I'd niver expect a hogger's son to stick wid the section gang."

"If I couldn't be in the cab," Randy told him, "I'd rather work for you than any place on the road. But I guess you know how it is."

"Sure, sure," Leary chuckled. "An' I'll be watchin' fer the wave o' yer hand whin ye ride past, so big an' fine! Here's wishin' ye luck, b'y!"

Randy didn't wait for the rest of the gang to arrive. He could tell Mike Hubka some other time. Just then he didn't want to talk, for the old section boss had given him a choked-up feeling.

He went back to town and strolled along the streets until

it was time to go to the big railroad office-building. At nine he was in the doctor's ante-room. The medical examiner of the mountain division was a spry, white-haired little man who handled a good-sized general practice in addition to his railroad duties. He took a quick look at the Master Mechanic's letter and his old eyes twinkled behind his spectacles.

"Randall MacDougal, eh?" he murmured. "Seems to me I recall signing a birth certificate for you, young feller. A pretty husky specimen you were, too. Eight pounds, ten ounces, or close to that. Well, let's see if you're man enough to fire an engine."

Randy stripped to the waist and had his chest thumped and stethoscoped. The doctor looked into his throat, asked him a few questions about diseases and fractures, and told him to put his shirt on again. "Now for the really important part," he said. "Eyes and ears."

He tested Randy's sight at various distances, covering first one of his eyes and then the other. "Twenty-twenty vision," he announced crisply. "Even the Air Forces'll take eyes like that. Come over here and pick the red yarns out o' that mess."

A skein of yarns of many colors hung on a hook. Randy

pulled half a dozen red ones from the hank and the physician nodded. "That'll do," he said. "Now the green ones."

The boy went through the same operation for green and then yellow. "Okay," the doctor told him, and wrote "Color vision normal" on the card he was filling out.

His hearing was the last thing to be checked. The doctor walked off several paces, turned his back, and told Randy to repeat after him whatever he said. He spoke in a low voice— "One—five—eleven—three—Washington—Pittsburgh—Gaptown." The performance was repeated with each of Randy's ears plugged in turn, and his hearing was pronounced excellent.

"Here you are, my boy," said the doctor, signing the card with a flourish. "I hope you do as well next door."

The rules examiner was quite a different type—a lean, hawk-faced individual who looked up at Randy sourly from behind his desk. At the farther end of the room two other young applicants were sucking their pencils over the written part of the examination.

The examiner read the letter Randy handed him and frowned. "What makes you think you want to be a fireman?" he snapped.

"I've always wanted to be one," said the boy simply. "My

father and two brothers are engineers."

Somewhat mollified, the man went on with his quiz. There were two or three easy questions on rules of the road, and some more difficult ones on train orders, automatic block signals, flagging, whistle signals and the like. "All right," said the examiner at last, "here's the written paper. You have half an hour to write the answers. Neatness and spelling will count."

Randy sat down with the sheet and looked it over. The questions covered principles of the steam engine, parts of a locomotive and a few other things which he had known almost since he could walk. But he was ordinarily an awkward penman and spelling had never been his strong point. So he took most of the half hour writing his answers as neatly as he could and pausing to spell each word over in his head before he put it down.

When he finished, the other two boys had already left. He signed the paper and handed it to the examiner, still uncertain as to whether he had passed. The man picked up a blue pencil, ready to pounce on each error. But though he scowled at the answers through his bifocals, he made only one mark at the bottom—a grudging "100."

"You can take this back to the Master Mechanic," said

the examiner testily. "Tell him to frame it. He doesn't get many like that."

Outside, in the busy street, Randy tried not to run. It was an exceptionally fine morning, he decided, and Gaptown had never looked half so beautiful before. Every time he passed a railroad man he squared his shoulders and straightened up to his full height. For he was one of them now—a real locomotive fireman.

Mr. Halliday was away from the office when Randy arrived but the girl clerk recognized him and nodded a greeting. "How did it go?" she asked. "All right, I hope, because our extra board is getting mighty short of names."

He grinned and passed over the medical card and the test paper. The young lady's eyes opened wide. "Whew!" she exclaimed. "I'll say you did all right! And I know the boss will be pleased. I think I can promise your name will be on the board before night. By the way, Mr.—ah—MacDougal, what's your telephone number, so we can call you?"

Randy explained that they lived on a farm out of town and didn't have a telephone. "Dad's got a regular run," he said, "so he comes down every day an' doesn't have to be called."

She tapped her teeth with her pencil. "That's too bad,"

she told him. "As an extra you'll be taking runs at all kinds of hours. Most of our men have telephones or live in boarding-houses so handy that the call-boy can reach them in a few minutes."

"Gee, I hadn't thought about that," said Randy, suddenly downcast. "But we'll do something right quick. I'll come down first thing in the morning an' let you know."

He hurried over to the roundhouse hoping to find his father, but old 722 had just started doubleheading a freight over the hump and wouldn't be back for another two hours.

A lot of the sunshine seemed to have gone out of the morning as he started the walk toward home. He could have saved time by jumping a freight but he didn't want to get his Sunday suit dirty. So he tramped up the road until a friendly truck-driver gave him a lift.

When he got to the house his mother was baking pies. She looked up quickly and saw dejection on his face. "Better change those clothes," she said. "By the time ye come down these'll be done and ye can have a bite. Ought to be good—made with the first o' the green apples."

He grinned and put an arm around her ample waist. "It's not as bad as that, Mom," he said. "I passed all right. Only maybe I'll have to move downtown to a boarding-house, so I can be on call."

"Indeed ye'll not!" she flashed. "Your father already thought o' that. Go look yon, in the front room."

Randy sprang through the doorway. There, on the corner table, sat a shiny new telephone.

"Gosh, Mom!" he yelled. "How'd you do it? I thought there was a shortage o' telephones these days!"

She was beaming. " 'Twas easy," she said, "when your father told 'em ye'd need it in a job essential to the war!"

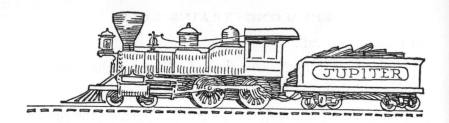

The locomotive fireman's job was never an easy one. In the oldest prints you can see him, shirt-sleeved but wearing a tall beaver hat, straddling the gap between engine and tender and heaving cordwood sticks into the firebox. When coal became the universal fuel he developed brawny muscles by constant use of the shovel and slice bar. Even today, when most of the main-line engines are oil-burners or equipped with automatic stokers, many a tallowpot still sweats out his time with a coal scoop. But he does it gladly, for he is on the only path that leads to the right-hand side of the cab. Ahead of him is a goal worth working for—the day when he can take the throttle as an engineer.

XVII

Randy lost no time in calling up the Master Mechanic's office and telling the girl clerk he could be reached by telephone.

"Somebody'll always be here," he said. "Any time you've got a run open—days, nights or Sundays—just call that number an' I'll be down in twenty minutes!"

She was amused at his eagerness. "You work fast, don't you?" she laughed. "It's only been two hours since you told me you didn't have a telephone! Well, Mr. Halliday's having your name lettered right now, to go up on the board. You'd better come down and see it."

He got out of his dress-up clothes and climbed into something that more befitted a fireman. Heavy work shoes, jeans and a "thousand-mile" blue shirt made up his costume. He tried on one of his father's high-crowned caps of striped drill, but it was too big for him. As soon as he had eaten a generous wedge of apple pie he swaggered down the path to the tracks and swung aboard an eastbound freight.

When he jumped off at the lower end of the yard he turned toward the business section. There was a railroad outfitting store on Main Street where they sold every kind of clothes, hats, gloves and shoes worn by train crews. It was while he was standing in front of the wide window, admiring the display of garments, that he saw the reflection of a bulbous figure in rumpled white linen coming up behind him.

"Well, well," said Ben Small's squeaky voice. "I was just wondering where I'd find you, my boy. Got a call from K. P. Harrow this morning."

The fat detective glanced up and down the street to make sure nobody was within hearing. "They've found a wrecked car up in Clearfield County," he went on in a lowered voice. "Ford sedan. It had run off the road into a pole and the front end was badly smashed. No sign of the driver anywhere around, but he'd left his finger-prints on the wheel. They were the same prints as the ones Harrow got from that notebook."

"You mean—Lew Burns'?" Randy asked.

Small nodded. "Only, of course, his name's not Burns. They nailed that down at headquarters in Washington. He's a German—naturalized citizen. Got his papers three years ago, and the name he gave then was Bruns—Ludwig Bruns. A pretty unpleasant character all 'round. I doubt if he'll bother you again, though, because he must know by this time that we've got the notebook."

"Just the same," said Randy, "I hope he's caught before long. There are too many things he could do to tie up the railroad."

He told Small about his new job and the detective congratulated him. "Maybe I'll be riding with you some time," smiled the fat man as he strolled away.

Randy went into the store and purchased a striped cotton cap like his father's. In front of the mirror he pulled the long visor rakishly over one eye and batted the full crown over sidewise. He was tempted to buy a pair of yellow leather gauntlet gloves but decided that would be an extravagance. His hands had been well toughened by his work on the section gang and he wasn't afraid of handling a coal scoop.

When he reached the Master Mechanic's office he had a proud moment. His name, neatly painted on a clean, white strip of cardboard, was in the bottom slot of the firemen's extra board. He stood there looking at it with a pounding heart and wondering how soon his chance would come.

The girl behind the counter tried not to show her amusement. "Oh, Mr. MacDougal," she called to him, "Mr. Halliday said he wanted to see you when you came in."

He went through the gate and approached the big desk with some trepidation. The big, white-haired man glanced up from under beetling brows.

"Well," he said, "you're on the board, young feller. No tellin' how soon you'll get a call, though, an' I figger you might as well be learnin' an' gettin' paid. So report to Sam Murdoch in the roundhouse tomorrow mornin'. He'll like nothin' better than breakin' in a MacDougal."

Randy thanked him and went out. He knew Old Man Murdoch by reputation—as crusty a curmudgeon as ever took the hide off a green mechanic. The news that he was going to work in the roundhouse was somewhat of a damper on his enthusiasm.

His father took a different view when he heard about it that evening. "Verra good," he nodded approvingly. "It'll do ye no harm to work around the engines a bit before ye ride the cab. An' deescipline never hurt a lad."

Randy rode down in the car next morning and accompanied his father to the roundhouse. There were at least twenty locomotives inside at that hour, but several already had steam up, ready for their runs. The engineer led the way across a maze of tracks and hose connections to the tiny office of the roundhouse foreman.

"Sam," he announced, as he threw open the door, "here's the new student fireman Halliday wants you to break in."

Then he turned and strode away, leaving Randy to face Murdoch alone. The old foreman looked ferocious enough as he swung about to stare at the boy. He had a bony face, decorated with a tremendous, drooping, white mustache above a grim, tight-lipped mouth. His cap was pushed far back on a head as bald as an egg.

"So!" he said tartly. "Think ye're a fireman, eh? Well, ye ain't—not yit. 'Round here ye're nothin' but a green punk, an' don't fergit it. When I tell ye I want an engine cleaned, it's gotta be *clean*—so I kin rub a white glove over it an' not smudge the fingers. When I tell ye to fill an oil-cup I don't want a drop spilled. There's a hog out here on Number 7 track, just in from four days on the road. Come on with me an' I'll show ye what's to be done to her."

He stalked out to the engine—a big Mountain-type 4-8-4— and pointed at it dramatically. "Look at that! A disgrace, she is—all soot an' cinders. Ye'll start up here at the head-light an' work back. Wash her down, wipe her off, shine her up. Here's the hose. The waste's back there in that box. 'Waste' is its name, but mind ye don't waste it! I'll be back here in two hours an' see what's been done."

Randy didn't say a word. But inwardly he vowed he would make the old fellow break down and praise the work he did. He went over to the box and got himself a handful of clean cotton waste. Another hostler, a small, middle-aged colored man, was there at the same time. He winked at Randy solemnly:

"Don' be skeert of him," the Negro whispered. "He mek a mighty big noise but he ain' half as bad as he soun'."

The days Randy had spent in the roundhouse when he was a big-eyed kid stood him in good stead now. He had seen too many engines washed down to be wholly ignorant of how to go about it. And though he was a bit clumsy at first, he watched how the colored man worked and imitated his movements.

It was a wet and dirty business, but he had expected that. In a way he began to enjoy it. Up there on the footboard, stretching his arms to wipe around the stack and the sand dome, he got a new idea of the iron brute's gigantic proportions. The fire had been drawn two hours before, and the great curve of the jacket was already cool, but deep in the boiler the steam still hissed and sighed gently. It was as if he were grooming a huge animal that made purring sounds of pleasure under his hands.

He kept at it steadily, scrubbing down the sides of the jacket, the smokebox and pilot, then working back along the cylinders, the mighty rods and the six-foot drive-wheels. He had reached the piping above the firebox when Sam Murdoch appeared beside him. The old man's mustache quivered as he squinted closely at the steel monster. He passed a gnarled hand along the under surface of a connecting-rod and examined his finger-tips. Then he went around to the other side, pausing for frequent inspections. Randy kept right on with what he was doing and braced himself for the blast he thought was sure to come. But as Murdoch passed him on the way back to his office, all he heard was a muffled "hrrumph."

The colored man on the next engine was doubled up with silent mirth. He winked at Randy once more. "Never said a mumblin' word!" he whispered. "Not a mumblin' word!"

The boy was glad he had saved the cab till the last. He got some clean waste and rubbed down the hand bars till they were spotless. Then he hoisted himself up into the gangway and drew a deep breath as he gazed at the engineer's seat—the throttle handle—the gleaming valves and gauges—the air-brake lever and all the other gadgets on the right-hand side

of the cab.

Across to the left was the domain of the fireman. That job would be a cinch, Randy thought, in a modern freight-hauler like this one. The huge firebox was fueled by an automatic coal-stoker. He could see the feed apparatus where it came up through the floor just under the fire-door. Its operation was controlled by the turn of a valve, and when it was working right the ashcat could loll on his seat and watch the track from the window. Of course, the boy remembered, automatic machinery didn't always perform the way it was supposed to. If anything went wrong the fireman would surely earn his pay, coaling that monster by hand.

He went over the interior of the cab lovingly, wiping the glass gauges and metalwork and the worn leather cushions. There wasn't much dirt there, for the driver and his fireman were evidently good housekeepers.

Just as he was finishing the job, the roundhouse foreman came clambering into the cab. He was still silent as his hawklike eyes inspected the results of Randy's labors. Finally his steel-trap mouth opened a crack. "I guess maybe you like engines," he said. "Sit down."

He motioned to the fireman's seat and perched himself

behind the throttle. "Ever done any firin'?" he asked.

"Not yet," Randy replied.

"Won't hurt ye none to know somethin' about it," the old man went on. "Now take a hand balmer like you'll be startin' on. Lots o' green hands think they have to keep that firebox full right up to the top. 'Tain't so. Ye'll kill a head o' steam quicker with too much coal than not enough. What ye got to learn is to keep yer ashes down an' clean o' clinkers. Then spread a good, even fire. Every shovelful ye throw, see that it spreads thin an' even. Then ye won't have no dead spots. First thing ye have to learn is to watch that steam gauge. It's your job to keep the needle pointin' straight up. The hogger, he'll take care o' the injector that keeps water in the b'iler. But makin' steam out of it is up to you. All right, come back in the shop with me. We got a set o' burnt-out drive-wheel bearin's to fix."

From that moment Sam Murdoch was like a different person. He handed out friendly advice on all manner of subjects, and even smiled once or twice. Something in Randy's eager willingness had broken down his reserve and given him an almost fatherly interest in helping the young railroader make good.

Before the week was out Randy was familiar with the

routine of the roundhouse. He was given some oiling to do and learned the trick of repacking a journal-box. One afternoon when a giant J-type 2-10-4 locomotive came in off the mountain run, Murdoch beckoned to him to get into the cab. The regular crew had run the big engine on the turntable and departed. Randy stood in the gangway and watched the foreman swing the table till the tender was opposite an empty stall track. Then Murdoch came to join him. The Negro hostler was grinning up at them from the ground.

"Goin' to let ye back her in," said the old man casually, and Randy's heart skipped a beat.

"There's your reverse." The foreman pointed. "You got a hundred an' eighty pounds o' steam—that's plenty. Easy does it now."

The boy's hand shook in spite of all his efforts, but he opened the throttle gently and felt the monster move under him. Yard by yard he let it creep back till he heard the pony wheels click clear of the table. The colored man signaled a warning from up ahead.

"Little more—'bout ten feet," Murdoch told him coolly. "Got to have her pilot back out o' the way. Easy—there ye are. Good enough."

Randy drew a deep breath and leaned out the cab window. The whole 115-foot length of locomotive and tender was on the stall track, but the rear coupler was only a yard from the bumper at the end of the rails. A slip of his hand on the throttle or the airbrake lever and they would have been through the roundhouse wall. It made him feel proud that the old man had trusted him for that delicate job.

As he got down, the colored hostler was chuckling to himself. "Sho' is a mighty good thing they didn' build that engine no bigger!" he said. "Reckon they must ha' measured the roun'house first. Yo' is a real runner, son, an' no foolin'!"

It was only on rare occasions that Randy's job gave him any such thrill as that one. For the most part it was hard, monotonous work. But he was learning something useful every day, and he knew Mr. Halliday had been right when he sent him there.

Still he couldn't help wishing for the day when he would really fire an engine, out on the road. One week went by and then another, and at last he saw his name in second place on the extra board. It wouldn't be long now, he thought. Probably it would be his luck to get his first assignment on some grubby little switch-engine—one of the yard goats.

The telephone rang one evening about nine o'clock, just

as Randy was getting ready for bed. His father answered it. When he had hung up he called to the boy from the foot of the stairs.

" 'Twas Buck Weeks," he rumbled. "Found a letter from his draft board when he got home tonight. He'll be off tomorrow an' he tells me your name is top o' the board. Will ye be ready to fire 722, the morn?"

The iron trail has a language of its own. Without regard for international boundaries, railroad men from Vancouver to Key West, from San Diego to Halifax, speak a common tongue so packed with picturesque slang that few ordinary people understand it. The words are short, expressive, pungent of coal smoke and lubricating oil. They are pass-words in the closely guarded fraternity of the rails.

XVIII

The hostlers already had steam up in 722's boiler when Randy and his father got to the roundhouse that morning. Old Sam Murdoch hurried out to greet them.

"I've heard the news," he snapped. "Looks like I'm losin' a good man just about the time he's worth his salt. Well, I ain't goin' to hold him back. You take him, Mac—only remember, he ain't ever done any real firin' yet. You got to teach him what he don't know, an' don't be too rough on him."

Big Ross grinned as the old fellow stalked back to his office. "Fine words, those," he said, "comin' from the toughest old browbeater on the division! Come on, lad, an' make the rounds wi' me while I oil her."

He took his long-nosed copper oilcan and filled it under the spigot of a barrel that stood by the wall. Then he made the circuit of the locomotive, jabbing the spout into hidden corners, giving Randy a running fire of comment as he went.

When he finished he sent the boy to Murdoch's office. "Tell him ye want the butterfly," he said.

The "butterfly" was the engineer's order without which no hogger could take his engine out. It was ready for them— a simple order to take the siding and wait for Special 21, coming in westbound on Track Three. They were to doublehead her through the Gap and wait for return orders.

Randy found he had a touch of stage fright when he swung up into the cab. Everything seemed to be going nicely. The indicator showed a good head of steam and the big freight-hog handled easily when his father rolled her off the turntable and into the yard. But the idea that he was responsible for keeping power in the 200-ton brute scared the boy at first.

He opened the fire-door for a quick look, and found the coal spread evenly and burning bright. Under his feet he could hear the steady rumble of the fuel moving through the stoker chute.

"Are ye catchin' those signals?" Big Ross called to him.

He remembered, then, that an important part of his job was to check signals and call them to the engineer. He leaned out the cab window and saw a switchman beckoning at the next crossover, a hundred yards ahead.

"Switch clear," he shouted, and his father grunted "Clear," in response.

They angled across to the siding and pulled in to wait for the special. Ross MacDougal looked at his watch. "Five minutes before she's due," he said. "Think ye can make the couplin'? There's verra little to it. About all ye'll have to do is hook up the air hose. Just give me a slow signal when I'm ten feet away, an' I'll do the rest."

Special 21, a long string of empty tank-cars, came in on time. Randy opened the siding switch while his father backed out, then closed it again. Next he ran back to the engine at the head of the freight and got the hogger's signal to couple on. His father eased 722 down the track at four or five miles an hour till Randy gave a downward motion with his hands. The big engine slowed to a crawl and the boy lined up the couplings and opened the jaws. Then, at his signal, the couplings clicked shut with hardly a jolt. As soon as his father had eased ahead to make sure they were fast, the boy joined the air hose and went forward to the cab. Most of his nervousness was gone now. Somehow doing that first simple job had made him sure of himself. He was a full-fledged tallowpot!

The three lights on the automatic block signal ahead changed position from diagonal to vertical and Randy reported that they had a clear track. His father leaned from the cab with one hand on the throttle and waved to the other engineer. The two locomotives puffed together in perfect unison. There was a gentle jerk as the drivers began to turn and then the long train was moving, gathering momentum as they hit the foot of the grade. It was a masterly piece of throttle work. Randy began to appreciate why Big Ross had been taken off the through runs and given this job. He was proud of his father.

That was an exhilarating day. Although the stoker took care of the coaling satisfactorily, Randy found he had plenty of duties to keep him busy. The steam pressure was down when they uncoupled on the other side of the mountain and he spent the half-hour wait in shaking down the fire and breaking up clinkers with the slice bar. His father helped with an occasional word of advice.

"A fire's no so verra different from a woman," he told the boy. "Ye've got to be firm wi' 'em both, but never rough."

Between watching his gauges and keeping an eye on the track, the boy had little time that day for looking at the scenery. But once or twice, on their half dozen round-trips over the crest, he glanced up at the towering cliff above the curve and felt a crawling in his stomach. He knew it was only by a twist of fortune that the whole mountainside was not now spread across the tracks. The soldiers were on guard up there, and it wasn't likely that a second attempt would be made to blast away the cliff-top. Still it gave him a twinge of apprehension when he remembered that the most dangerous of the saboteurs had never been caught.

He wondered where Burns was now. Hiding out somewhere in the neighborhood, perhaps, and plotting further deviltry. But this was too fine a summer day to spend worrying about Burns. White clouds drifted high in clear blue air above Big Calico's mighty dome, and the gorge of the Blacksnake was full of purple shadows. The whole main line, or at least the ten miles of it that he could see from the mountain's shoulder, was crowded with trains. They were running so close that 722 had been bucking a "slow-board" most of the afternoon—throttled back, waiting for the signal to change at every block. Randy had the feeling, as never before, of being in the very middle of the nation's biggest job.

They were on the outside track, eastbound at the head end of a string of yellow "reefers"—refrigerated fruit express cars from California. Big Ross had told his son, while they were waiting to tie on, that this would be the last run of the day for 722. Randy caught the clear signal at the head of the grade and they started the long coast down around the curve, part of which was still hidden by the bulge of the mountain. The boy glanced at his gauges, opened the fire-door to see how the coal was burning, and went back to his seat by the window.

His view of the track ahead unrolled steadily as the train rounded the hill. Off to the right, past the nose of the engine, the tree-clad side of the gorge fell away sheer to the river, hundreds of feet below. Suddenly Randy gave a startled jump.

"Dad!" he yelled. "There's a flag ahead!"

A quarter of a mile down the track a dot of red had come into view—a tiny dot waved by a frightened brakeman who looked no bigger than an ant. It was still hidden from his father, riding the right-hand seatbox on the outside of the curve. But Big Ross acted instantly at that call. He slammed the air lever over and reached for the whistle valve.

The warning hoot was answered by a blast from the road engine behind, and Randy, looking back, saw that the other fireman had also sighted the flag. The heavy train slowed jerkily as the binders took hold. When they ground to a stop, 722 had passed the flagman, and the caboose of the stalled train was in sight ahead.

The elderly brakeman, still short of breath from his run up the grade, came past, rolling up the red flag.

"What's up?" Randy asked him, trying to sound professionally offhand.

"Huh? Dunno, son," the shack replied. "Emergency stop. Torpedoes. Must be another train tied up somewhere down below."

Just then they heard five short whistle-blasts from around the hill—the signal calling in the flagman.

"Well, so long now," said the brakie. "That's for me. Got to get back to the crummy." And he jogged off toward his train.

"That was a quick one," Big Ross growled. "Hardly worth the wear an' tear o' stoppin' us. We'll wait till they've got a good start an' follow on slow till we can see the whole grade."

Five minutes later they were well around the hill and into the crescent of the big curve. The train ahead of them was two miles ahead, rolling smoothly, making up time.

They made the yard without further incident and Randy uncoupled. The tallowpot aboard the road hog leaned out his window and hailed him. "What was wrong with 33?"

he asked. "Did that shack give you the dope?"

"Not much," said Randy. "He told me it was a torpedo stop, but that doesn't make much sense. Nothing wrong with the track an' the next two blocks were clear."

"Somebody must be nuts." The other fireman grinned. "Well, be seein' you, kid." And the train of reefers rolled on its way.

Big Ross ran 722 in on the turntable and climbed down, but Randy waited in the gangway till his friend the colored hostler arrived.

"Okay, Rufus," he said grandly, "you can take her away now. See she gets a good scrub-down an' I want that bright-work nice an' shiny—"

He had to duck at that point to avoid the ball of wet waste the Negro flung at his head.

Back in the washroom he found an argument in progress. Two of the "home guard"—engineers with seniority, who came in off regular day runs at the same time as his father— were discussing the emergency stop made by the 33 freight.

"It's these wild kids," old Eddie Smith was insisting. "Parents don't pay a mite of attention to 'em these days. Just let 'em run loose. It'd be easy enough fer 'em to git hold of a dynamite cap, or even a reg'lar rail torpedo. Then the whole line jams up fer five minutes an' a lot o' cars git flat wheels from a smoky stop. I say they ought to be took home an' have the daylights whaled out of 'em.''

"Maybe that driver on 33 only *thought* he heard torpedoes," another engineer put in. "I got fooled one time like that. 'Twas in rabbit season—fall o' the year. There was a hunter down in some brush beside the track an' I didn't see him. First I knew I heard a *bang—bang*, an' I put the Johnson bar in the deep hole. Sure did feel silly when the 'brains' got done ridin' me!"

Big Ross frowned and shook his head. "There's verra few rabbit gunners about in August," he answered. "I'm thinkin' it's one o' those things ye can't explain. Queer enough, but no great harm done. Weel, wash yersel', lad, an' let's be goin'."

They found Jeannie waiting in the car.

"How's the big-shot fireman?" she asked. "He didn't wreck your precious engine, did he, Dad?"

"No." Big Ross smiled. "He did a verra fair job—even saved a collision, ye might say. Did it strike ye, lad, that whoever put out those torpedoes picked a mean spot? On a left-hand curve around a mountain the engineer is blind as a bat."

Randy nodded soberly. "I was thinking the same thing," he said.

It was after dark that evening when the telephone rang. Big Ross had already gone upstairs and Randy answered.

"This is Buck Weeks," said the voice on the phone. "Your father around?"

"I think he's gone to bed, Buck," the boy told him. "Any message I can give him? How'd you come out at the draft board?"

"I'm in, all right," the fireman answered. "The doc said I was sound as a dollar. Got three weeks to put my affairs in order, such as they are. Reckon I'll stick with the job till I go, so tell your dad I'll be with him in the morning."

"Okay," said Randy. "I figured my luck was too good to last when they gave me your run today."

Weeks laughed. "Oh, well," he replied, "soon as I go you'll have a clear track. Say—wait a minute—I almost forgot to tell you. Did you folks hear the news? There's been a bad freight wreck down near Harrisburg. They say all four tracks are blocked an' it'll be midnight before they can get it cleaned up."

"Gosh!" said Randy, lowering his voice so that his mother wouldn't hear. "Anybody killed?"

"One brakeman—don't know his name, but he was an old-timer. They were rollin' right up to the speed limit, makin' up their time, an' a journal burned out, somewhere in the middle o' the train. Axle broke an' pitched that car an' twenty more all over the right-o'-way. Some o' the boys heard a kind of a rumor about that journal-box. They say they found it half full o' sand!"

"That's bad," Randy murmured. "Sounds as if it was done on purpose. What train was it—do you know?"

"Yeah," said Buck. "It was Number 33."

When America went to war there was every expectation that we would be bombed by the enemy from the air. Civilian defense volunteers were organized and air spotting posts were manned in thousands of cities and hamlets. Meanwhile the huge new munitions plants we needed were built on prairie soil, deep in the mid-section of the continent, where they would be out of reach of Axis planes. But the products of those plants had to be used on overseas fronts—hundreds of millions of pounds of them. That is why you may have seen boxcars on the main freight lines to tidewater bearing the warning card: "EXPLOSIVES."

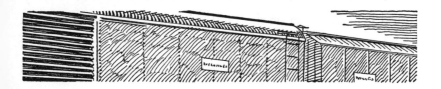

XIX

Randy told his father the news before breakfast next morning. Big Ross was not a talkative man and it was sometimes hard to tell what he was thinking. But watching his black brows knit, the boy could see he didn't like what he heard.

"I figured maybe that stop they made at the top o' the grade might have something to do with it," said Randy, guardedly. "What do you think, Dad?"

"Maybe. Maybe not." The engineer's voice was gruff. "What'll ye be doin', now Buck's back on his run?"

"Reckon I'll go down with you an' work in the roundhouse till I'm called. That is—if Sam Murdoch wants me."

Big Ross nodded. "He'll be wantin' ye. No doubt o' that."

Around the Gaptown Yard there was little else discussed but the wreck of the 33 freight, that morning. Engineers and firemen, switchmen, section hands and roundhouse hostlers all had their own versions of the affair, and Randy found it hard to get at the facts. But there was one point on which nearly all agreed. The journal hadn't burned out from ordinary causes—lack of grease or bad packing. There was something special about that hot-box. It was the double handful of sand in it that had ground the axle through.

Old Sam Murdoch seemed glad to see his apprentice fireman back. He was working on the whistle of an antiquated passenger locomotive, and he initiated Randy into the mysteries of whistle tone.

"This here's off old Number 61," he explained. "She was the pride o' the road forty-five year ago. Light-built an' trim, with them four high drive-wheels ye used to see on her type. She couldn't pull much weight on a grade but once she got up speed on a level track she'd go like a scalded cat. Nowadays she's on a little local run up an' down the valley branch. Old Jake Kiekheffer's her engineer—treats her like a lady. He complains her voice ain't what it was, an' the valley folks like to set their clocks by her, so he asked me to do some tinkerin'. Listen."

He had a steam pipe rigged to the work-bench, and when he turned the valve a hoarse, asthmatic croak burst from the whistle. It made Randy jump a foot.

"Gosh!" he said. "Pretty awful, isn't it?"

The old man grinned. "Well, don't judge by that. Matter o' fact, I took her vocal cords out. Wait till I do a little fixin' an' you'll hear the sweetest triple-chime whistle this side o' the mountain."

He showed Randy a disc of thin, blackened brass, its edge worn and ragged. Set in the vise beside the whistle was another piece of metal, similar to the first in shape, but bright and clean-edged. Delicately the old foreman went to work on it with a file.

"Got to get her so she fits just right," he explained. Every few moments he removed the disc and measured it with his eye against the base of the whistle.

"That ought to do it," he said finally. "Let's put her in an' see what happens." He fitted a threaded bar through the hole in the center of the plate and screwed it down till there was only a hairsbreadth of space between its edge and the saucer-shaped base of the whistle. Then he put on the big cylinder with its three scalloped vents, and adjusted it over the disc. When he opened the steam valve the whistle poured out a deep, mellow chord that was like organ music.

"Oh, boy!" Randy gasped. "That's beautiful!"

Sam Murdoch wiped his hands. "Yep," he said. "She'll do. Ain't a sound in the world any purtier'n a good engine whistle. I reckon when ol' Gabriel blows his trump on the last day it'll be somethin' like that."

Randy was just finishing the last crumb of pie in his

lunch-box that noon, when the call-boy came into the round-house.

"Your name MacDougal?" he asked. "Got a call for you to take out a special freight at two o'clock. Bill Anson's the hogger. You goin' to take it?"

" 'Course I'll take it," Randy told him. "What's the run?"

"Westbound to Pittsburgh. Anson's reg'lar fireman'll be there, an' you'll have to deadhead back."

"That's okay with me. I'll be on deck."

Bill Anson came in about one-thirty. He was one of the younger engineers, but known on the division as a good man in the cab. He greeted Randy cordially.

"I hear you're goin' to fire for me this trip," he said. "You're dad says you did all right yesterday, but this engine o' mine's a hand-fired job. Think you can swing it?"

"Well, I'll never know till I try," the boy answered with a grin. "Matter o' fact, I've been wanting to find out."

They went over to the stall where the locomotive stood, and Anson started his oiling. A hostler had already fired up and the steam was rising in the gauge. Randy climbed to the cab and took a look at the fire. The door through which he would have to throw coal appeared alarmingly small, but the tender was full and there was a good shovel that felt right to his hands.

He opened the door and tried a couple of practice shots. The swing of the big scoop came naturally enough, and though the first shovelful scattered a few lumps of coal on the cab floor, the second was a bull's-eye.

A few minutes before two they ran the engine out of the roundhouse. A switcher had just finished making up a drag of seventy cars—mixed freight and empties—on one of the yard tracks. Anson backed up to the head end and Randy made the coupling. He had practiced the trick of it enough times so that he managed without difficulty.

Bill Anson tested the air, checked his orders with the conductor, and pulled out on the dot. The lead engine that doubleheaded them up the grade was 722. Buck Weeks leaned out the left-hand window and gave Randy a cheerful hail.

"All right, kid," Anson sang out. "It's a tough haul up to the Gap an' I'm goin' to need plenty o' steam."

Randy saw the gauge had dropped a point or two below the 200 mark. He grabbed the shovel and opened the firebox door. He knew he had to work fast, for he could keep the door open only a few seconds at a time without cooling off the arch. Bracing his feet in the gangway and swinging from the hips, he threw six big scoopfuls of coal into the twelve-foot firebox. Then he slammed the door and watched the indicator. He knew he had spread the coal well over the fire and left a roaring red space at the front. It ought to work, and it did. A minute or two later the hand on the steam gauge was climbing again.

"Good boy!" Anson called to him. "You do that every couple o' minutes an' we'll be over the mountain 'fore you know it."

Between pouring coal and watching the signals, Randy put in a busy half hour. Once they were over the hump and the helper engine had cut off, the pulling was a little easier. But even so the boy got all the exercise he could ask. Long before the five-hour run to Pittsburgh was over, the muscles in his back, arms and shoulders had begun complaining.

The Pittsburgh yards marked the end of the division, and another engine took over at that point. Anson ran his locomotive onto a spare track where several others were already standing.

"Well, kid," said the engineer, "you made a first-class run. If I didn't know better, I'd think you'd had a month firin' hand-balmers. My orders are to lay over here till tomorrow, an' pick up an eastbound freight. My tallowpot's waitin'

here for me, but if you want to ride back with us you're welcome."

"Thanks," Randy said, "but I'd better get on home. I told Dad I'd be back before morning. I'll just hop the next through freight that comes along."

He made his way across the yard, threading a maze of crowded tracks, and asked a switchman where he could get something to eat.

"You're a railroader," said the man. "Most of us like Mamie's place, over next to the Yard Office. It ain't fancy but the chow's good an' the prices reasonable. Mame'll take care of any guy with coal dust on his face."

Randy's hand went up to his cheek involuntarily and the switchman chuckled as he walked away. It wasn't till he found the little restaurant and sat down on one of the counter stools that the boy realized just how grimy his trip had made him. In the long mirror behind the counter a coal-blackened visage under a fireman's cap looked back at him with startled eyes.

Mamie was a big, red-haired Irishwoman with a loud and cheerful laugh. She cooked with one hand, served with the other, and kept up a running fire of banter with the men who were eating.

"What'll it be, dearie?" she asked Randy, cleaning the counter in front of him with a deft swipe of her cloth. "The beef stew's good tonight, an' there's a sink out back if ye'd like to scrub up a bit."

When he returned, with face washed clean, there was a big plate of stew, bread and butter and a cup of coffee waiting for him. He went to work on them with a hungry boy's appetite, winding up his meal with a generous wedge of blueberry pie.

Just as he reached in his pocket for money to pay his check, a broad-shouldered young railroad man swung down on the stool beside him. It was Joe Roan.

"Well, doggone!" cried the brakeman delightedly. "I heard you were firin', Randy, but I sure didn't expect to run into you in Pittsburgh. Where you headin' from here?"

Randy explained about his trip west with Anson. "I'm trying to catch a freight home tonight," he said. "Which way are you bound?"

"We pull out for Gaptown an' points east in forty minutes," Roan told him. "Come on an' ride in our crummy. I'm on the hind-end tonight, so I'll be 'round to keep you company."

It was an ideal arrangement from Randy's standpoint. He

waited while the freight shack put away a hearty supper, then went with him on a stroll through the nearer streets of the big town. Randy had been in Pittsburgh before, but he bought a picture post-card of the railroad station and mailed it to Stan Lukowski with a "wish you were here" message.

Darkness was near when they returned to the yard. Joe Roan led the way over to his train and back along the track to the caboose. Randy, walking behind him, saw that nearly half the boxcars carried those small, white cards that have a special meaning for railroad men—"Explosives: do not hump."

Roan ushered the boy into the crummy and introduced him to the conductor, an elderly, worried-looking man, busy over his way-bills. Assured by the "brains" that he was welcome to ride over the mountain, Randy tried to make himself useful. He helped the brakeman fill and set his marker lights and put coal on the fire in the little cook-stove. After the train got under way, they climbed up into the cupola together.

"You've got plenty o' hot cars up ahead tonight, Joe," Randy remarked.

"Yep," said Joe. "Plenty. They really packed this drag with the stuff. Oh, well—I've hauled so much of it now I don't mind any more'n I would if the cars were full o' potatoes.

"Say, tell me about catchin' those Nazi bums up on Calico. I heard part o' the story from Ben Small, but he admits he never got but halfway up there."

Randy laughed. "He did his best," he said, "but poor Ben just isn't cut out for mountain climbing. The thing didn't get in the papers, o' course. Those F.B.I. cases are generally kept quiet. We did catch two of 'em, though, when they were about ready to blow the top o' the cliff off. It wasn't much fun for me, because I had to run around in the rain with nothing on but a bunch o' leaves.

"You remember that guy Burns we chased into Bronsky's saloon once—the fellow that had the red notebook? Well, he was the brains o' the gang, an' he got away. Sometimes I have a feeling he's still around."

"You mean you think you've seen him?" asked Roan.

"No—but when queer things happen on the line, I kind of suspect he had a hand in 'em. Like that journal-box that wrecked the 33 freight above Harrisburg last night. Did you hear about that?"

"Yep," said the brakeman grimly. "There was some dirty work in that one, all right. An' I knew Wally Gates, the shack that got killed. A nice, harmless old gent. The conductor says every car in that train was inspected at Pittsburgh. It's hard to believe they'd miss a box full o' sand."

"That's right." Randy nodded. "But 33 was stopped three or four minutes at the top o' the big curve. We were right behind 'em an' it was Gates who came back an' flagged us. Three minutes would be plenty for a smart worker like Burns. An' you know they haven't found out yet who put those torpedoes on the track."

"Say—" Roan squirmed uneasily—"That's somethin' I hadn't heard about. Did you tell Ben Small?"

"I didn't have a chance. Anyhow, it's just a guess. Maybe I've got saboteurs on the brain."

They rode in silence for a while. Randy stretched his tired muscles and leaned back against the wall of the cupola.

"Go ahead," said Joe. "Catch yourself a little sleep. I've got to watch the train, but I'll wake you up before we get to the Gap."

The boy must have slept for several hours. It was the jolt of the coupling, when the helper engine tied on, that roused him. The brakeman had left the cupola, and a fragrant smell of coffee came up from the room below. Randy shook the stiffness out of his arms and legs and went down the ladder.

"Have a cup o' java?" the conductor invited him. "Gets sort o' cold, nights, up here in the mountains, so we keep a pot warmin' on the stove."

Randy accepted gratefully and was sipping the hot, black brew when the train clanked into motion and Joe Roan came aboard.

"Sure is frosty out there." He shivered, rubbing his hands. "Moon's up, though, an' it's a mighty pretty night. You tore off a good nap, didn't you, kid? Feel better?"

"I feel swell." Randy grinned. "With a cupful o' this stuff in me I could lick my weight in wildcats."

The deep, barking exhaust of the two engines came back to them as they labored up the grade. Randy and Joe finished their coffee and climbed back to their perch in the top of the caboose. Neither of them had much to say. It was enough to sit there and take in the shadowy beauty of the night—the mist and the moonlight and the vast black shapes of the sleeping mountains.

They crossed the saddle of the Gap and started down around the shoulder of Big Calico, looming tremendous on their left. To the right lay the abyss of Blacksnake Gorge, a bottomless pit that writhed with silvery wisps of vapor.

Suddenly Randy was thrown forward with a jerk.

"Emergency stop!" Roan growled. "He sure threw the air to her in a hurry. I gotta get out a flare an' do some flaggin'!"

The motion of the train was slowing rapidly as Randy followed his friend down the ladder. The conductor looked alarmed.

"Be sure you don't flag short," he urged Roan. "Remember we're on a curve here. You better jump right now an' start runnin'."

Randy's heart was pounding as he went back to the rear platform. This was almost the same spot where the 33 freight had been halted, and something told him it was more than a coincidence. But he had no time to talk to Joe about it. The brakeman was already down on the step, clinging to the handbar. "Good-by now!" he called cheerfully, and swung off into the dark.

Thirty yards more and the train jolted to a stop.

"I'm going up ahead," Randy called to the conductor. Then he was pounding along on the ballast beside the cars —the right side—the outside—because he was still following a hunch. The way the moonlight fell, it was the right side of the train that was in shadow.

He had been running at top speed for more than a minute

when he saw the light. A quick, faint flash, a dozen cars ahead—then darkness again. It was down at the level of the wheels. Staring at the place as he ran, he thought there was a darker shadow there, close in against the side of the car.

It was very quiet on the mountain, now that the train had stopped. Randy tried to go silently but bits of rock crunched under his racing feet. The shadow, only a dozen yards away now, changed shape suddenly. A man straightened up, looked over his shoulder, then darted for the bank. Randy didn't hesitate. Winded as he was, he took off in a flying jump, aiming, feet first, for the figure scrambling down the slope.

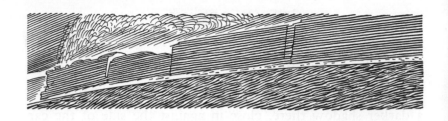

Some time you may ride west in a crack passenger express across the Alleghenies. Around midnight you'll wake to a changed rhythm in the rolling of the wheels, a muffled chugging of powerful engines. You'll pull up the shade in your sleeper and look out. Then you'll recognize the big curve, and the gorge, and Calico Gap, even though those aren't their real names. Perhaps you'll hear the wailing hoot of a freight locomotive thundering down the grade. And you can say, "There's an old friend. That's Randy MacDougal's hand on the whistle valve!"

XX

The side of the gorge was steep as the pitch of a roof, and Randy's leap carried him twenty feet downward. His heavy work shoes caught the fleeing man squarely between the shoulders and knocked him headlong into a tree below. There was a breathless instant while the boy picked himself up. Then he was grappling, hand-to-hand, with a bulky figure that outweighed him by many pounds. There was just enough light to show Randy the gun in the man's right hand.

He seized the fellow's wrist and put forth all his strength to force the pistol muzzle outward, away from his head. And he was none too soon, for in that same second it was fired with a blinding flash, a foot from his face.

Still clutching the wrist, Randy swung his knee behind his adversary's and tripped him. They fell heavily, with the boy on top, and getting both hands into action he was able to twist the big automatic out of the man's grasp. There was no time to think. He lifted the gun by the muzzle and smashed it down savagely on the bare head beneath him. Once—twice—and the man lay still.

Randy staggered to his feet, gasping for breath. He wasn't taking any chances. The fellow might be playing 'possum. He backed off a yard or two and kept his finger on the trigger of the pistol.

When he recovered enough of his wind, he shouted for help and thought he heard a distant answer. He waited and yelled again, his voice echoing back eerily from Blacksnake Mountain across the valley.

After a moment there was a noise of hurrying footsteps on the track above. "Hey! Where are you? What's the trouble?" someone called.

"I'm down here. Bring a flashlight," the boy answered. And shortly he was joined by the conductor and the head-end brakeman.

"I reckon here's the guy that stopped your train," said Randy. "Let's see what he looks like."

The conductor swung the beam of his light toward the crumpled figure on the ground, and Randy saw the heavy body and pale, distorted face of Lew Burns.

He felt his knees go weak. "Is—is he dead?" he whispered.

The brakeman put an ear to Burns' chest. "Nope," he said. "Heart's still beatin'. He'll live to hang yet."

Amongst them, they dragged the saboteur up to the track,

and Randy told the conductor what he had seen. "It was right about here," he said. "Looked as if he was fooling with a journal-box."

They examined the boxes of half a dozen cars and found two with sand in them.

"Okay," the conductor told his shack. "Tell that hogger to ease her down slow an' take a side track in the yard. He'll have to call in Roan first. An' have him pull up here so we can load this so-an'-so aboard the crummy."

Burns was still unconscious when the caboose drew abreast of them and stopped. Joe Roan helped them carry him inside and tie him up.

"Well, kid," the brakeman told Randy, "seems to me you've had quite a night. You want to hop off, down the grade here, an' get home to bed? I'll take care o' your boyfriend."

Randy yawned. "All right," he said. "There isn't much more I can do tonight, I guess. Only I sort o' hate to miss seeing Ben Small's face when he finds out who we've got."

He went to the rear step and prepared to swing off when they reached the home path.

"So long," said Joe. "An'—an' don't forget to give my best to your sister!"

It was late in August when Gaptown celebrated Army Day. The whole city was gay with red-white-and-blue streamers, and cool, bright mountain weather brought crowds from far up and down the valley. Every railroad man who could be spared from the job was on hand with his family. At noon the public square in front of the courthouse was packed with people as it hadn't been in years.

Randy had a queer, proud feeling, sitting up there on the wooden platform behind the flags and the bunting. Stan Lukowski was beside him and they were both uneasy in their best clothes. There were a lot of others on the platform—Mr. Harrow, the G-man, and some soldiers with ribbons on their breasts, and a big, bronzed Major General, seated by the Mayor. But it was the crowd down in the square that Randy watched.

He could see his father's great shoulders and his mother's face, strong and happy, and Jeannie, with Joe Roan close to her side. Old Dan Leary was there with a grin on his wide Irish mouth, and Mike Hubka, and Mrs. Lukowski, and Mr. Halliday, the Master Mechanic, and Sam Murdoch, and Rufus, the colored roundhouse hostler.

The Mayor was on his feet now and everybody else got up with him, as the band played "The Star-Spangled Banner." Then pretty soon the Major General was speaking. He had a gruff, short way with words but he knew what he was talking about.

"This is a railroad town," he said. "I'm proud to come back here and talk to railroad men and women. You don't do much bragging. You don't have time. But the job you're doing in this war is something the country ought to hear about.

"How do they think the biggest supply of war equipment in the history of the world got from the factories to the docks? How do they think we got ten million men into training camps and most of them overseas with their supplies—eight tons of supplies for every man, and another ton a month as long as he's fighting?

"You've done that job. You and all the other railroad people in America. You've done it shorthanded, because I've seen a lot of your best young men in uniform, slugging it out with Japs and Nazis on twenty different fronts.

"Two of them, I'm glad to say, are here with me on the platform. They've been running locomotives on supply lines in North Africa and in India—under pretty tough conditions, I might add. Now they're home on furlough and I'm going to introduce them. I think perhaps you'll recognize their names. First Lieutenant Robert MacDougal and Technical Sergeant James MacDougal, of Gaptown, Pennsylvania!"

Randy nearly fell off his chair. The two soldiers had come from the station in a car with the General and marched up to the platform behind him. This was the first time he had had a good look at them.

"Gosh!" whispered Stan. "Are they your brothers?"

Randy nodded, still speechless.

"And now," said the General, when the mighty wave of applause had died down, "it's my privilege to present two other young men—fighters on the home front. Most of you know the story of what they did. Without their loyalty and courage there might be no trains running over this main line today. Randall MacDougal, of Gaptown, and Stanley Lukowski, of Doran—please come forward."

The two boys stumbled to their feet and walked to the front of the platform amid a storm of cheers. The General saluted smartly, then shook hands with each of them in turn. His face was solemn but there was a twinkle in his eye.

"In behalf of the Army of the United States and its Commander-in-Chief," he said, "I thank you both."

Randy never could remember just what happened next. He was aware of the band playing, and Bob and Jim hugging him. A moment later K. P. Harrow was shaking his hand.

"Put this in your pocket." The F.B.I. man smiled. "It's your part of the reward. You and Stan get five hundred apiece." And he slipped a folded check into the boy's fist.

Then Big Ross MacDougal had somehow climbed the platform, pulling his stout wife up after him. "Weel," he boomed, " 'tis the greatest day the MacDougals ever knew." And he swept the whole clan into his bearlike embrace.

Randy's mother cried a little. It was the first time he had ever seen her cry, but these were tears of joy.

"All my lads," she said. "All my big lads safe. But there! What am I moonin' about? The dinner's still to be cooked! Ross—Robert—James—Randy—come wi' me, now. Jeannie, fetch the car. Let me think. There's chickens to fry, an' string beans an' carrots an' early potatoes, an' I'll make hot biscuits to eat wi' honey, an' blueberry pie—"

They all laughed at her as she counted off the items on her plump fingers.

"Mom, you're wonderful," said Bob.

And Randy and the rest agreed.